Ghost Swamp Blues

Ghost Swamp Blues

Laraine Herring

White River Press
Amherst, Massachusetts

First published June 2010

White River Press
P.O. Box 3561
Amherst, MA 01004

www.whiteriverpress.com

Printed in the United States of America

ISBN: 978-1-935052-27-2

Book and cover design by The Concentrium
www.theconcentrium.com

This is a work of fiction. All characters, events, and dialogue are
imagined and not intended to represent real people, living or dead.

Library of Congress Cataloging-in-Publication Data

Herring, Laraine, 1968-
Ghost swamp blues / by Laraine Herring.
p. cm.
ISBN 978-1-935052-27-2
1. Race relations--Fiction. 2. North Carolina--Fiction. I. Title.
PS3608.E7755G48 2010
813'.6--dc22
2010005621

for dad

The murdered do haunt their murderers, I believe.
I know that ghosts have wandered on earth.
Be with me always -- take any form -- drive me mad!
Only do not leave me in this abyss, where I cannot find you!

Emily Brontë – Wuthering Heights

1
The Single Step

Roberta Du Bois

The sun was unusually hot for October on that morning in 1859 when I walked into Snaky Swamp, just south of our rice plantation in Alderman, North Carolina, wearing nothing but my pink feathered hat. The water was thick as wool and it clung to my skin like a net. Moccasin snakes swam near me, skirting the top of the water, their eyes and fangs cracking the surface. I wiggled my toes in the soft mud of the swamp floor until the weight of the marsh was too much and my toes stopped moving. I walked forward into the swamp until my legs stopped lifting and I fell forward, my cheek hitting the water with a slap before sinking sinking into the blanket of algae and mosses, branches and vines, their tentacles covering my nostrils, wrapping my jaw tightly closed, my teeth fitted perfectly together until my skin fell away in clumps for the fish.

On the day of my death, my husband, Jonathan du Bois, ordered one of his slaves, my half sister Claudia, whipped. The overseer poured salt onto her open back and I screamed from the silence of the marsh. Claudia's eyes rolled in her skull and her tongue dripped saliva onto the earth.

On the day of my death, talk of an uprising was beginning. A man named Douglass was going to be the next Moses. Jonathan believed it and took to craziness. Our plantation, our livelihood, depended entirely on the men and women who worked our rice fields. We depended entirely on that human property of ours, bought and paid for with United States currency, now sweating under the Carolina sun.

Idyllic Grove Rice Plantation, as I knew it, has long since returned to the swamp. It's me who's still around. Poking in and around the tall pines, crunching my feet over the dried pinecones just enough to make you jump. Me who drips clear water down the hallway, my nakedness shivering in the air. The house that's there now, in the very spot where our big house used to be, is a five-room clapboard with a black shingled roof. The property has been divided and divided and divided until nobody knows who owned what or whom or even why much anymore. The clapboard house is on about a hundred acres of woods and bottomlands, bordered to the west by Snaky Swamp.

The folks who live there, Lillian and Hannah Green, keep a really nice garden in the back by the septic tank. They grow corn and tomatoes and butter beans and even okra. The soil is gray loose sand that washes away when the hurricanes come. There are shells here now, brought from trips to Wrightsville Beach, and a rusted green chair out by the back steps that sometimes shelters a white cat. It's been almost one hundred and twenty years, and to people driving by in their motorcars on the new paved street, everything is as it should be. Beautiful land, a carpet of pine needles and leaves, a quiet house overlooking the water. Idyllic.

But I still smell the broken bodies and bloody hearts. I press myself into the walls of this clapboard house and the vibrations are there still and again, still and again. When I dissolve through the walls into their living room with the single square of gray carpet in front of the fireplace, I see not Lillian and Hannah moving about, but the others: The shadow figures draped in blue with empty eye sockets and twisted fingers. The little girls dancing in white flowing dresses.

Ring around the rosies
Pocket full of posies
Ashes, ashes, we all fall down!

The men, backs arched forward, arms over their heads swaying like reeds beside the swamp. The grinding sound of the wagon wheels plodding through the wet clay earth. The mosquitoes, big as big toes, swarming around the algae-coated water. All of this I see, through eyes that never close. All of this wraps around my mind like satin ribbon, one layer at a time.

When I walked into Snaky Swamp I fully expected that would be the end of it. At least the end of it for Roberta du Bois, daughter of Thomas Saunders, wife of Jonathan du Bois, mistress of Idyllic Grove rice plantation. I had no idea it would just be the beginning of my story. Time looped around me, caught me in its square knot, and held me tight. Held me here. Watching all of this madness unfolding in front of me, unwinding like snakeskin, dragging everyone along.

I see others like me walking this property. It is an odd place though. I see them. They see me. But most of us can't speak to one another. We can't touch each other. We can only pass by, feel the coolness from each other's paths, see the wildness in each other's eyes. The only ones I can talk to are the ones directly connected to my own sorrows, and sometimes all I want is for them to go on back to their own sadness and leave me be.

On the day that I walked into Snaky Swamp, I was eighteen years old. I had been married less than six months. I had no noble intentions. I wasn't protesting the plight of the Negroes. I wasn't lamenting my own role in the Southern society of oppression. I wasn't even mourning my own wretched marriage. It was the four girls, really, who called me into the water. The swamp sirens.

Over and over they sang their rhyme. The rosies. The posies. These little girls. Two white, golden hair flying around them like capes. Two black, hair full and wild on their heads as the four of them spun in endless circles just on the other side of the swamp from me.

Roberta! Play with us!
Oh, yes! Roberta, come dance with us!
Over here! Over here!
We'll wait for you!
Come! Just a little bit closer!

The little girls played on the sand bar in the middle of the swamp. You can't see the exact place anymore, but it was right over there where the pier ends now. They danced and danced. They came to my room and danced on the ceiling, carrying vines and pine knots. They danced in my dreams, bound together at the waist with snakes.

When we were little girls, Claudia and I used to dance with these four spirits. We both saw them, and when the six of us played together, we laughed as loud as the Carolina parakeets. Now I only see glimpses of them in the trees. A bit of a dark ankle. A strand of blonde hair entangled in a branch. A square of indigo fabric. A whisper in my ear when the ospreys take flight.

I have walked these acres for over a century trying to come up with the best way to tell my story to you. How to describe to you the slaves? The way it was for a white woman then? How to say these things to you without preaching, without being condescending, without telling you what to feel? The only solution I have come up with is just to tell you, and to hope that in the telling I can reach some truth. Perhaps the facts are wrong. Perhaps they never existed at all. It has been a long time. I am left with memory, unreliable in the best of times. I can only tell you what I know and how all this is wrapped up with Lillian and her daughter Hannah Green and Gabriel Wilson and Jay Transom and the mad boy Tommy Green in the crazy house up in Mecklenburg County. I can only hope you trust me enough to believe that what I'm telling you is truth.

2
Closed For Winter

Lillian Green
October 17, 1949

Yesterday didn't happen.

I pulled some of the batting out of my quilt and stuffed it in my ears so I wouldn't hear his sounds anymore.

But it didn't work.

I stood for over an hour in a scalding shower, but I couldn't wash the black boy's fingerprints off my wrist. They circled around my bone, knotted together where his thumb and middle finger had pressed, and settled in.

Lillian Green
October 16, 1949

My older brother Tommy was eighteen years old. I was fourteen, and I woke up especially early because Tommy said he'd take me to the ocean to watch the sailboats. I liked the ocean in the fall-time. We hadn't been to the beach together in a very long while. Tommy'd been busy being eighteen, and Daddy'd been busy trying to get elected mayor, and Mother'd been busy being lonely. I'd been busy being in the ninth grade trying not to notice the blonde-haired boy in my history class, but I was never too busy to go to the beach on a Saturday. Never.

We lived in Alderman, North Carolina, in a house that used to be a slave plantation house. Mother always reminded me this actual house wasn't the plantation house. That house got destroyed when the Civil War happened. But it felt like the old plantation house. The land around our house was deep and dark. Not scary dark though. Dark like when you are snuggled up under your quilt at night and you know in the morning there'll be eggs and biscuits and a trip to the ocean.

We had a swamp, too, that Mother told me not to go near, but I did anyway to watch the alligators. It's called Snaky Swamp, and Mother says lots of bad things happened by that swamp. I figured out a long time ago that grown-ups tell you stories about things to keep you from exploring, so I don't pay any attention to that at all. I loved to sit by the swamp and watch the water move. Sometimes an alligator eye cut across the water. Sometimes I saw a pair of snakes. Sometimes the water moved and I couldn't quite figure out why, because there's never a breeze at all down there.

Tommy wasn't at breakfast that morning. Daddy had already gone out to Beauford Country Club to play golf with his politics-friends. Mother always looked forward to Saturday breakfasts because she could spend time with her favorite child, Tommy, and I, her not-so-favorite child, could help her clean the drapes. But today, Tommy wasn't there, even though Mother made up his favorite omelet complete with sausage and yellow cheese and grits. She set his place at the table and then sat herself down in her regular chair next to Daddy's empty one.

"Reckon your brother must have had something more important to do today," she said. She held her white china coffee mug to her lips but did not drink. "He say anything to you?"

"No." I could tell where this day was going to go. Not only was I not going to get to go to the beach and watch the sailboats, but I was going to have to help Mother clean the drapes without Tommy's help getting them off the rods.

Mother and Tommy got on well. It was Daddy and Tommy what had all the problems. Daddy wanted a football player or somebody special smart who could help him run his campaign or work with him at the insurance company. But Tommy wasn't any of those things. Tommy liked to draw. He sketched anything he could see. Chairs, tables, beds. Sometimes, if he was feeling really friendly, he sketched Mother and me doing dishes. Tommy was born with pictures swimming around in his head. Daddy didn't approve though. Once he tore up a picture Tommy had drawn of Daddy for Father's Day. He wadded it right into a ball under Tommy's nose and threw it in the fireplace. I was only six then, but I could tell Tommy wanted to cry because of the way his arms shook. When I found him in his room later, after Daddy had told me how pretty my own Father's Day drawing was, he was curled into a ball, his colored pencils and paper thrown all over the gray carpet. Mother and Daddy fought that night, like they often did.

"Let the boy be," Mother said.

I couldn't hear anything from Daddy except curse words and the word "sissy." The fight ended like usual, with Daddy storming out of the house to sit in the driveway in the Ford Sportsman and smoke his Pall Malls. From my upstairs window, I could see the orange dot of the cigarette.

"Hey, Tommy, it's me," I said from the doorway. "Butter Bean." That was his special name for me. He said it was because I was thin and flat like butter beans. "Can I come in?"

His face was pressed into his pillow. "Go away!"

I stood in the doorway anyway, hoping he'd lift his head off the bed, but he never did.

I missed Tommy this morning. When the sun came through the dining room window just right, I would notice how handsome he was, with his orange hair and blue-like-the-ocean eyes, and I would know he would be a great man someday. Maybe even a famous artist, no matter what Daddy said. Sometimes, teasing, I'd pick on his gigantic flappy feet that Mother said he hadn't grown into yet. But not this morning. Just me and Mother this morning.

"Maybe he's meetin' him a girl!" Mother winked at me. I knew she and Daddy were worried Tommy hadn't found a girlfriend yet.

"I don't think Tommy wants to do that."

"Someday you'll understand," said Mother, this time drinking her coffee in one swallow.

That morning I helped Mother clean the house like always, only this time we didn't have Tommy's help for the high places. We dusted all the furniture, arranging the lace doilies over the shiny wood tables. We wore yellow rubber gloves and cleaned the toilet bowls with ammonia. Every other Saturday, we washed the windows, top to bottom, inside and out, Mother holding the ladder steady while I climbed to reach the highest corners. Tommy usually helped. I liked the feeling of knowing his hands were holding the sides of the ladder. It made me feel like he was lifting me up to heaven, and I felt safe knowing he was on the ground holding me steady, ready to catch me if I fell. But this Saturday we were on our own, and Mother's grip on the ladder wasn't as strong and the ladder swung from side to side as I reached for the corners of the windows.

Mother tried to pretend nothing was any different. She was an expert at that, always acting like things were fine. She had a knack for shaping whatever mess was in front of her to whatever way best suited her. Still, I kind of enjoyed spending the day alone with her. I always hoped she'd tell me something that could be our secret and we could giggle like best friends. But Mother was a closed-off room at the top of the stairs to me.

By the time Daddy came back from the country club, the house sparkled. He kissed Mother on the cheek.

"How was your game, dear?" she asked.

"Three under par." He set his golf bag down in the foyer. "Jimmy and I set a personal record." Daddy didn't pronounce "r's" unless they started the word. They rolled out of his mouth into vowels.

"That's wonderful, dear."

Daddy didn't notice how clean the house was. He walked over our polished floors with his outdoor shoes, leaving little pieces of dirt on the linoleum in the patterns of his soles. I watched Mother carefully, trying to see if she would put on her "face" for Daddy. She could do the most amazing things with her face. She became like a doll whenever she didn't want to talk about something. The corners of her mouth turned down. Her laugh lines around her mouth and eyes vanished. She clenched her jaw so her jawbone appeared sharp and angled, and she'd interlace her fingers tight like the stitches on Tommy's football. She could look right through you then.

But Mother didn't put the face on. When Daddy passed her, she whispered something in his ear, which made him stop and touch her cheek. When we sat down to supper, he even cut his own steak. We didn't talk about the empty place at the table. Mother had put out a plate and a cup full of milk like always for Tommy. Daddy tried to pretend that he wasn't mad but he gripped his silverware too tight.

"You sure Tommy didn't say anything to you, honey?" Mother asked me.

My mouth was full of pork peas. I shook my head.

"Well, I'm sure he'll be home soon."

Daddy set his fork down on the plate. "If he knows what's good for him."

I stared at my supper. The steak looked gray, the pork peas too green. I shifted in my chair. My feet still wouldn't reach the ground.

"Honey, I'm sure he'll be back." Mother spooned more peas on my plate.

"Mother, I don't want anymore."

"Mind your mother," said Daddy.

The meal continued in the kind of silence that falls thick as dust. The sun had set and the three of us were all reflected in the panes of the picture window, staring two feet in front of ourselves, shifting the food from one side of the plate to another. I don't know how long we all sat there like that, hypnotized by the window images of ourselves eating. Fork to mouth to plate and back to mouth again. The three of us moving in slow motion as if we were under water. Nobody looking at each other. Nobody touching each other. We just spooned food into our mouths and looked at Tommy's empty chair and pretended not to see it.

I had a piece of steak caught in my teeth that I was working on with my tongue. Ever so often I'd catch Daddy's eyes shifting nervously towards the window. He avoided Mother's gaze. I asked Mother could I be excused, but she just kept chewing her food, so I picked up my plate and carried it into the kitchen and sneaked up the back stairs to my room.

As soon as I closed my bedroom door, the shouting began. It was that low kind of shouting. The kind that is a single tone—no rising and falling—just one solitary note pulsing like the telltale heart across the bottom floor of our house. I tried, like I always did, not to hear it. I stuffed tissues in my ears. I practiced singing my scales for music class. I jumped on my bed as high as I could, almost hitting my head on the white ceiling. When I heard the dish break in the kitchen, I escaped. I opened the shade and lifted the window and climbed onto the branch of the oak tree that bumped up against the side of our house. It was cold; the night air wet, and my heart pounding from the broken dish, the low shouting, the absence of my brother and the leap from the window.

The earth under my feet was so soft I felt the whole world was sinking. Mother and Daddy's shadows danced in the picture window, faces close, bodies apart. I knew without seeing that Mother's lips were disappearing and that Daddy's mouth was getting bigger, his lips puffier and redder with his rage at Mother's silence. My shoelace had come untied and when I bent over to lace it back I saw Bernie, my favorite horny toad, blinking up at me from an old log. He hopped away as quick as he could, the rustling of the leaves in his path sounding just like an Eastern diamondback rattler, and I took off running.

The crunch of the tires from Tommy's truck on the loose gravel road sounded like bones breaking. Tiny rocks sprayed onto the sandy roadside. I jumped out of the way, scratching my legs in the bushes that grew in clumps along the road. I wasn't sure at first the truck was Tommy's. The moon was only a crescent, and the tiniest one at that. In daylight, Tommy's Ford pickup was a baby blue, speckled with red mud that dried to a dull brown around the running boards and doors. In darkness, it looked black. He drove without his headlights on and maybe it was because he kept the lights off that I was able to see the squirrel tail that flew off the radio antenna. The truck stopped just at the end of the road. I tried to remember what was down there. Was that where Mr. Wilson lived? Or was that where the creek took a turn toward the inland waterway? I crouched as low as I could, my elbows up to my chin, my fingers holding me together.

I inched forward, quiet as I could be. It was what was in the back of the pickup that stopped me from calling out to Tommy. It looked like a present you'd get at Christmas, a swing set or something like that, from Sears. Then it moved. There were three boys around it, passing bottles of something I thought must be beer. They were laughing and carrying on, ignoring the bundle between them. Tommy got out of the truck. I recognized the angle of his shoulders, hunched too far forward, ashamed, as always, of his height. The crickets were carrying on so loud I thought they had crawled right up in my ears and were singing to the back of my skull. The bundle in the pickup bed twisted into an "s" shape, reminding me of the time daddy caught a copperhead in the backyard and put it in a burlap sack. The snake scurried across the grass in the darkness of the sack until daddy could get the garden shovel and crush its skull. Maybe Tommy had caught a huge snake. There were stories all the time about the creatures that lived in Snaky Swamp, great stories about monsters and dragons and ghosts of pirates. Maybe Tommy had caught an alligator. That had to be it. The bundle was really too big for a snake. Even I knew that.

Then I heard the noise. At first it was so soft I could have told myself I didn't hear it at all. Then there could be no doubt.

Fabric ripping.

Knife plunging into some soft, sticky substance. One of Tommy's friends falling, hitting the back of his head on a rock in the ground. Bare black foot emerging from the pickup bed. White wrists wrapped around the foot. Man emerging from sack, unfolding like a paper doll.

Tommy, holding a rope, standing by a tree. Not enough moonlight to see his eyes. Man shivering, surrounded by a circle of white boys. No sheets. No horses or crosses. Just boys. With ropes. And knives. And clubs.

And laughter.

Eenie, meenie, miney mo.

Catch a nigger by the toe.

Owl cried. Thud of wood on bone. Man on his knees.

Thud. Man on the ground. Curled tight. Crack!

Tommy, standing. Tommy, watching.

Owl.

Screaming. I am screaming but with no sound. My mouth is open.

No noise. No noise. Where is the noise?

Crack! Cry out. Beg.

Crack! Fall. Thud not so loud now.

Dragging.

Dragging a man sounds like burrowing.

Tommy, standing.

Snake in the tree! Snake in the tree beside Tommy!

I am screaming! Hear me!

If he hollers, let him go.

Hear me!

I fall on my knees.

Man lifted up. Limp. Tommy puts the man's head in the snake circle.

Man cries.

Jesus! Sweet Jesus!

Boys laugh. Ooga booga. You pray to your voodoo gods. What business Jesus have with nigger trash like you.

Hear me! Oh, God! I'm screaming but I'm not screaming.

JESUS!

Snap!

Panting, heavy breath. Dog breath. Swimming through thick thick air to break through on the other side. Run! Run!

Tommy, nodding. Tightening the snake loop around the man's neck.

Tommy, smiling. Drop him.

Heavy. Snake becomes a rope. Tightening.

Hanging, hanging, lord, lord.

Lordlordlordlordlordlordlordlordlordlordlordlordlordlord.

I am frozen. Vines wrap around my ankles. Hold me in place. Keep me away. Mouth open. No sound. No screaming. Eyes open. Eyes open.

help

help

help

let him go oh let him go

Laughing. Tossing a pinecone around the circle. Man hanging. Snake around his neck. Feet twitching. Not dead.

let him go

Tommy shrugging shoulders. Patting backs.

The only good nigger, he says.

A dead nigger, they shout.

Laughter.

Vines snap from around my ankles. Fall forward.

Who's there?

No noise. Mouth open.

Who's there?

tommytommytommytommy please stop it

Someone's here!

Scramble. Boys in pickup bed. Gravel flying.

Truck backs up. License plate six inches from my nose. Black on yellow. North Carolina 49, number 238-497.

Tires squealing. Gravel spray peppers my cheek.

Man hanging.

Owl sound.

No noise.

Breath stopped.

Mouth closed.

No noise.

Mouth.

Closed.

I kept my face pressed into the sand as long as I could. I felt as if I weren't wearing any clothes. The dampness chilled me, shook my teeth against themselves in a rattle. Then the branch broke. Cut through the silence like a shotgun. I screamed and the sound of my own voice startled me more than the sound coming from beneath the tree.

I began to walk, wobbling on my own ankles. I was panting now, no longer able to scream, my tongue fat in my mouth. I couldn't hear Tommy's pickup anymore, only the sound of my own feet on the dried leaves, heavy as elephant steps. I crossed the road and stopped suddenly when I reached the pile of human flesh and bones. A dark liquid dripped from his mouth, forming a puddle beside his head. His eyes were open and he made a gurgling sound from deep in his chest.

"Are you alive?" I whispered. I tried to see if his chest was moving. It was hard to tell in the darkness and from the way he had folded when he fell from the tree. I wanted to touch him and run away at the same time. My chest was full of sounds I did not make. The body on the ground lay twisted into itself, legs at forty-five degree angles to either side. I wanted both to believe I saw him move and that he was dead at the same time. His eyes opened and I must have jumped back a yard and a half. My chest was so full of screaming I didn't know how to let it out. He was a boy like Tommy. Just a boy. I crept as close to the body as I dared. "I'll get help." But before I could decide which way to run, he raised his right hand up and grabbed my wrist.

"Tell..." He sputtered the word at me and his hand fell from my arm. He was dead for keeps this time. I looked around to see if anything was lying around that belonged to Tommy. I knew sooner or later somebody would come by and find the body. I swallowed and stuffed what I saw deep into my belly and walked toward home.

I don't know what time of night or early morning it was when I climbed back up the tree and shimmied into my bedroom. The ground was damp and everything seemed very very still. The swamp frogs called to each other and I couldn't shake the feeling that when the sun came up my whole world was going to be in different colors than I remembered it. A mist hung low to the ground and the salt smell from the ocean coated my nostrils. No leaf rustled in the trees. No car drove by on the main road. I could have easily been the only person alive in all of Alderman. I kept looking over my shoulder, hoping I'd see Tommy come driving up. I needed to talk to him before he got inside. But he never came.

Lillian Green
October 18, 1949

Tommy stayed gone. I felt somehow Daddy knew what had happened, and strangely enough, didn't much care. Mother, on the other hand, hadn't eaten a bite of food; she just kept vigil at the dining room table, looking out the picture window waiting for her boy to come back. Since nobody seemed to notice me at all, I pretty much stayed up in my room, picking at the threads on my quilt, trying to stuff the batting I'd pulled out back in, unraveling squares at the bottom where I hoped no one would notice. Daddy knocked on my door the second morning and when I said, "Come in," he opened the door, entered, and just gazed out into the room. I had half a square of purple velvet in my hand.

"Your mother's not going to be too happy with you destroying that quilt. You know that's been in the family for generations."

"Yes, sir."

"Reckon you're old enough to know better."

"Yes, sir."

"You know anything about where your brother is? If you do, now is the time to let me know."

I squeezed the fabric, ripping more of the stitches from the quilt.

Daddy sat on the bed next to me and slowly separated my fingers from the velvet, uncurling each one, pressing it out flat like a paper note. "Did you climb out of your bedroom window night before last?"

"No, sir."

"There's never any shame in telling the truth."

Maybe it wasn't Tommy driving his pickup truck. Maybe he loaned it to a buddy who just looked like Tommy in the dark. Maybe I just had one of those really bizarre dreams where you actually feel wet if it's raining or cold if it's snowing. Maybe I didn't crawl out of my bedroom window and walk down through the woods and see Tommy and his friends beating a black body to death in the dark. I just couldn't have. Because if I did, my brother Tommy was gone forever.

October 20, 1949

It was three more days before Tommy drove back in the driveway, young red facial hair sprouting from his chin, eyes a vacant blue. By that time, the boy's body had been found by a young black child playing hide-and-seek in the woods, and an old darkness moved through our house. The body's name was Gabriel Wilson and he lived over by the Cape Fear River at the docks. He had a sister named Minnie and a cousin named Jay who was only a few years older than me and was "pale enough to be white" according to the papers. He was only seventeen. "Unknown persons" killed him, according to the paper; the details claimed he was apparently "beaten and hanged until dead." The police had no comment.

When Tommy did walk back through the door, there was a great deal of carrying on about him, like he was the Prodigal Son or something even bigger. Tommy and Daddy took their rifles and went out into the woods one morning and were gone clear past sunset. Mother wouldn't say anything about it other than wasn't it nice for the two men to spend a little time together. I'd never heard Tommy referred to as a man before, and it sounded false, like the noises of the caged animals at the zoo.

I hung around the house trying to help Mother with the cleaning or the cooking. Tommy hadn't looked at me once since he'd been back. I knew I'd been avoiding his gaze too, but I thought surely he'd want to talk to me. He'd grabbed the back of my head the first day he was back and rubbed my scalp. "How ya doin', Butter Bean?" But he didn't really stay long enough for me to answer, and I don't know how I could have replied anyway.

By the time he asked me how I was doing, I had already begun to stop talking. Interestingly enough, nobody noticed at all. The first morning I played a game with myself. I wanted to see how long I could go without saying a word before anyone figured it out and made me speak. Turned out the only thing Mother said was how nice it was that I was being so quiet. So I went on to day two of my game, completely certain that someone would make me speak by that point. I guess it was a good thing I didn't have anyone to bet with. Mother loved my silence and Daddy had never paid much attention anyway.

Moment by moment, the fact that I saw my brother kill that black boy dissolved into smoky shadows that grew large in moonlight and disappeared completely in daylight. Soon, I could pretend as well as Mother that nothing bad had happened.

There was a funeral for the black body named Gabriel Wilson at the black Baptist church on the other side of the creek. The national news came all the way from New York to do a feature about lynching. They talked about Gabriel Wilson and also about the other eleven black men who had been lynched in the past year. Daddy was furious that a Northerner could come down to our town and pretend he knew anything about anything. The Negroes marched. The whites marched. Firebombs went off like Fourth of July fireworks. The Klan men rode their horses in the night. The police found no information leading to the murderers of Gabriel Wilson and the case was officially closed fourteen days after the body had been found.

Tommy listened to the news on the radio and stroked the stubble on his chin. He didn't flinch at the mention of the body's name. He didn't shift in his chair when they spoke of the riots. When I watched him, I heard his voice saying "the only good nigger" over and over in my head. Tommy, what happened? Tommy, what did you do to us? To yourself? To Gabriel Wilson? Why won't you talk to me? Why don't you notice I am not talking to you?

Daddy and Tommy spent a great deal of time whispering together. Mother and I now ate our Saturday breakfasts by ourselves. Mother always made a little extra bacon or a few more pancakes in case Tommy dropped in, but he never did. One morning she asked me, "What is going on with your brother? Didn't he tell you anything?"

I shook my head. He didn't twirl me around his head in the backyard anymore. He didn't rub my head and call me Butter Bean. He didn't sneak up on me when I was in the bathroom and make me jump so I'd squirt toothpaste all over my blouse. He most certainly did not tell me a thing.

"I declare, he's just not been himself." Mother wiped the frying pan with a blue and white dishcloth. "I look at him at supper and I don't even recognize him." She snapped the dishcloth at me. "Get on out of here and play. You shouldn't be listening to your mother carry on like this."

I nodded and slid off the chair.

Right before the investigation wrapped up, Tommy locked himself in his room for six days. Daddy went in to visit him every few hours or so. Mother stayed downstairs in the kitchen, slamming pots and pans and occasionally crying like Mary at the foot of the cross. I hadn't been out of my room much either. I had nightmares. Long loopy ones that always began and ended at the same place—a ragged rope swinging in the moonlight.

Before that night, my worst nightmare had been about jellybeans. Jellybeans had danced round and round the highest part of my bedroom walls. They laughed and sang and multiplied over and over again until the whole room was filled with them and I couldn't breathe. I saw them even after I woke up. Mother and Daddy didn't believe me and talked to me like I was a baby, but I knew they were really there, multicolored and full of sugar, waiting to swallow me up.

When Daddy went into Tommy's room, he would shout. I never heard Tommy say anything back. One morning, I thought I heard a piece of furniture crash against the wall, but I never found anything broken when I sneaked into Tommy's room after he'd left us to go to that special place in Mecklenburg County.

Sheriff Paterson had been to our house twice since the night I saw what happened. Daddy invited him into his den for scotch and man-talk. When he left, Sheriff Paterson slapped Daddy on the back like they were both football players, and Daddy let out a tiny laugh that sounded so desperate my insides hurt.

Sheriff Paterson put his big sheriff hat on and winked. "We'll take care of it, Mr. Green. We'll get this investigation closed right up."

Daddy nodded. "Thank you, kindly."

"Tommy's a good boy. It'll be all right. And I sure appreciate your offer."

I sat on the staircase, my arms wrapped around the railing. Daddy looked at his wingtips. "Say hello to the wife, Sheriff."

"Will do."

Daddy walked past me on his way up the stairs to Tommy's room. I don't know if he even saw me. His neck was a strange purple color. Mother was still in the kitchen scouring the pans. Daddy yelled some more from inside Tommy's room. When he came back downstairs, he went straight to the study and slammed the door. Mother emerged from the kitchen, wiping her hands on her paisley print apron.

"Was that your father?"

I nodded.

"Where's your brother?"

I pointed upstairs. Mother grunted and went back into the kitchen. I sat on the stairs as long as I could. I had to go to the bathroom, but I held on to the pain in my bladder until the heavy pressing felt as natural as breathing.

On the sixth day after what I saw, Tommy walked out of his room. I was lying on my bed arranging paper dolls. He didn't look in my room at all. I leapt from the bed, scattering my dolls on the floor, and followed him down the stairs. He was so lanky; I thought he must have lost twenty pounds in those six days. Daddy hadn't been to work in a week. Mother's eyes were thin paper cuts in her drawn face. They both sat at the kitchen table, staring at empty plates. When Tommy got to the foot of the stairs, they looked up. Mother ran to him, hugged him and then slapped him. Daddy stayed in his chair. Tommy turned to me, and I saw eyes I'd never seen.

"Hey, Butter Bean," he whispered.

I stayed back, afraid to come close to him. He knelt on one knee. He doesn't know, I realized. He doesn't know I saw him. My teeth felt pointy against my tongue.

"Butter Bean. Don't be that way."

Tommy, my Tommy! I watched the sailboats on the ocean with you. I used to feel so tall on your shoulders. You held me higher than the branches where you strung that boy. I ran to him, shaking against his chest.

"Shhh," he said. "I'm going to be fine."

Eenie meenie miney mo

That boy Gabriel Wilson isn't going to be fine. I'm not going to be fine.

I pressed my lips against his ear. "Why?"

He pushed me away like I was fire. He didn't speak. I saw a flicker of the eyes I knew just one week ago, but he blinked too quickly and the light went out.

I used to think the only ghost in our house was the sheet Daddy hung in the back of his closet. When I was little, I would pull it off its wooden hanger and drape it over my body. I could never get the eyeholes to line up right with my tiny head, so I would fall down the stairs a lot in the darkness and land, white and giggling, at Mother's feet.

3
Darkness

Gabriel Wilson
1949

The woods animals knew what was coming before I heard the engine. I'd been just walking along the road, kicking up a little sand with the toe of my boot, when the rumbling of the engine emerged like the growling of a mountain lion behind me. Next thing I heard was laughing. The voices sounded so young, I let my guard down for just a minute, thinking they must be kids like me. Fatal mistake. They were kids. And they weren't like me one bit.

I came to Tommy in a cloud of smoke the next day. The kind of smoke you get when you burn your trash in the backyard. He never heard me. He didn't see me. I've been hanging on his shoulder ever since. He thinks I'll go away. He thinks with enough praying and screaming and twisting his quilt into knots I'll go away.

But I have nowhere to go.

Some folks call me the devil. But that's the fool's way out. Those who hate me most got me living in their bones.

4
The Absence of Boats

Lillian Green
1951

In the beginning, I really believed somebody was going to come along and make me start talking. I thought—I hoped—that Mother and Daddy missed me talking at dinner or missed me telling them all about what stories we read in school that day, but Tommy broke them. Once he left us for the crazy house in Mecklenburg County, they stopped talking even to each other and silence became my new brother.

Things I never heard before became loud. Sounds like Mother flicking out her dishrag over the sink, the spatters of water slapping the faucet. Sounds like Daddy pushing the mower around the yard in random patterns. Sounds like leaves falling and ice melting and telephones not ringing and the preacher not stopping by. We filled our whole house with silence so big it pushed at the walls, blowing the curtains out the wrong way, as if sending an SOS to the world. I'd come home from school, books tied together with one of Daddy's belts, and I'd see the curtains waving at me, long arms of burgundy velvet, and I'd wave back at my friend in the walls.

I saw Tommy, or rather the absence of Tommy, everywhere, most often in the way I was becoming absent, right in front of everyone's eyes, but no one except the house noticed. I turned sixteen with no sounds at all.

One Saturday in March, a week after my silent sixteenth birthday, Mother came into my room.

"Put on your Sunday dress, Lillian. We're going to see Tommy today."

She stood in the doorway for a moment. I could have responded to her, but I didn't. It had been a year since we had visited Tommy. Daddy was downstairs turning the pages of the newspaper loudly. Mother's upper lip looked like the inverted "v" of geese flying south. She'd gotten glasses since Tommy went away—black cat's eye frames with a rhinestone on each arm. To me, they made her eyes look that much farther away.

I pulled out my white and blue polka dot dress with the crinolines and laid it on the bed. Inside, I felt like my stomach moved into my throat, literally swallowing up any words I might have been able to say. I saw the boy body Gabriel Wilson right in front of me on my very own quilt. I saw Tommy's squirrel tail and then I heard the thud of the stick on the body's back and my own back quivered. I wanted to stay here in Tommy's old dress shirt knotted sloppily at my waist and listen.

It was almost a six-hour drive to Charlotte State Hospital, formerly Charlotte Hospital for the Insane. They changed the name in 1946, but from what I remember, not much else changed. Men and women were often chained up, sometimes to each other. People were submerged in ice water and shocked. One ancient Civil War veteran still walked the halls. He claimed he was the oldest man alive, and from the looks of him, his body was older than flesh should be allowed to get. He had no teeth and his hair stood up in three white stalks. His skin folded into itself, and his left arm was missing. The nurses called him "Old Jim" and let him be. Soon, he'd be in the cemetery west of the building.

Dust from the road blew onto my dress and Mother's tightly curled, clipped back hair wilted from the humidity. Daddy kept his right arm on the steering wheel the entire way, his arm stiff as a tree. His left arm dangled loosely out the window as if it had no connection whatever to the other arm. Mother pointed out flowers along the way. I sat in the backseat, my ponytail touching the place between my shoulder blades no one had touched, refusing to sit on

Tommy's side of the car. The Plymouth Suburban was new—a 1951 —and it was way too big for the three of us. Silence took up the rest of the space in the wagon, pressing down on our necks and squeezing our wrists. I dropped peanuts in my Coca-Cola bottle and drank deep and belched, just to annoy Mother.

The Charlotte State Hospital was kudzu-covered, the vines looping across the iron barred windows, even crossing over the sidewalks.

"The vine that ate the South," Mother said, stepping carefully over an entanglement.

"It's good for the soil," said Daddy. "Prevents erosion."

I thought it looked like it held the hospital in a big green hug, something natural to hold the unnatural things going on inside. I wondered if Tommy ever thought about reaching through the bars, grabbing one of the vines, and letting it pull him out, at a foot a day, until he was free.

Tommy was in the dining hall in a straight-backed chair. He wasn't chained up. He wasn't wet from ice water. But he was silent —almost as silent as me. Daddy poured a cup of water from a tin pitcher and sat across from him. Mother stood as straight as a corn stalk, both gloved hands holding her small clutch purse. I stared at his hands. He'd bitten all his nails practically off. The skin was shredded, dotted with dried blood.

"Good to see you, son," Daddy said.

Tommy took Daddy's cup of water, drank it, but said nothing.

Mother nodded at Daddy, who handed Tommy a black case with a handle. I hadn't noticed Daddy had brought anything in. Tommy opened the clasp. A Zenith portable radio! Tommy twisted one of the black dials. Underneath were four red buttons – one for treble, one for voice, one for alto and one for bass. The dials looked like what I imagined an airplane cockpit would be like. My eyes narrowed. We didn't have one this nice at home.

"I thought you might like to listen to the baseball," Mother said. "I thought it might make you feel better."

"Thank you, Mother," he said, his voice a frog. "I sure will enjoy it."

"Are you having any trouble, son?" Daddy asked.

"No, sir. I'm doing fine."

I noticed Tommy didn't raise his gaze to meet Daddy's. Instead, he glanced around the empty dining hall, as if he were being followed.

"Are you sure? I can have a talk with someone."

"I'm fine."

My crinolines itched. Tommy grabbed my hand as I knelt to scratch behind my knees. "Hey, Butter Bean."

I nodded, unwilling to give him my voice.

"Hope you're doing good in school."

I nodded.

"She seems to not talk so much," Mother said. She waved her gloved hand in the air. "It's just a phase, I'm sure."

"That must be right," Tommy said, but he didn't release my hand. I wanted to pull away from him. He held as tightly as he must have held the stick that beat the boy body Gabriel Wilson in the sack. Held as tightly as I thought he held me when we went to the ocean to watch the boats. He couldn't hold on to me anymore, I realized. I had gone someplace else and I knew that even if his hand held my wrist in the exact same spot the black boy's fingers had touched, I could move out the windows, out over the kudzu and the cemetery, back onto the highway and head east. I didn't need anyone to be with me anymore. "There's something with me," he said into my ear. "Something trying to kill me inside."

I shook his hand off.

"Lillian! Your brother misses you," said Mother.

"It's OK, Mother. Butter Bean's just in a mood today." He tried to smile like old times up at Mother, but all of us knew it was someone else's smile. Maybe the smile of that something that was with him. Maybe the smile of the body of Gabriel Wilson. Whoever's smile it was, it wasn't Tommy's. Had we used Mother's sewing scissors and clipped him out of all our perfectly posed family portraits, we couldn't have left him more completely. He belonged to something else now.

"We best be heading back, son. Tomorrow's church," said Daddy.

"Yes, sir."

"You go to services here, Tommy," said Mother. "Just listen to it." She kissed the top of his head. "Just listen to it."

"Yes, Mother."

Daddy picked up his hat and the three of us left him there, alone at the dining room table, ear pressed to the Zenith.

September 18, 1965

On the swing I sat
Looking for my cat
Mommy came to play
Chased him far away
I don't know her name
But I see her just the same
Running through the house
Quiet as a mouse
Mommy doesn't see her
Or she seems afraid to meet her
But at night she visits me
Up in the branches of my tree
It isn't hard to see her
Open your eyes and greet her
But she lives inside the walls
Crying lonely ghostly calls.

Hannah Green, age 7

5
Ways of Not Speaking

Roberta du Bois

It was my father who sold me to Jonathan du Bois. Only I don't know what my father got, except rid of me. Jonathan got a handsome dowry, a bride, and four more slaves, one of whom was my half sister Claudia, another her mother Annie. He also got the unspoken political connection my father could provide him for his bid for Congress. They were both very happy men.

My own mother tried to tell me I could do a lot worse. While she twisted my hair into French knots and forced abalone combs into it, she told me more with her jerking, pulling motions than with her words.

"He has the largest plantation in the county," she said. "You'll be well taken care of. You're lucky to be marrying so well so young." A hairpin fell to the floor. When she stooped to pick it up, I heard her sigh.

"You're glad Claudia and Annie are coming with me," I said.

"I don't deny it. How would you feel, every day seeing the child your husband fathered with another woman? A nigger woman! Just how would you feel?"

"I imagine I'll know soon enough, though I don't think I'll care who Jonathan takes a liking to."

"You wait and see, child. You'll care. Whether you care or not." Mother slid the last of the hairpins in at the nape of my neck. "You look beautiful. Jonathan will be here any minute now. He'll be pleased."

I didn't care if Jonathan was pleased or not. I was grateful Claudia and Annie could come with me, but that was all. The way we were that afternoon, my mother and I standing in front of the vanity in my childhood bedroom, my young eighteen-year-old face in front of her older one, was the best it ever was between us. She knew what she was sending me to, and there was nothing she could do about it, and I like to pretend it made her sad. I saw a shimmer of water in her eyes behind the glint from her spectacles and chose to call that love.

"Roberta, the best you can hope for is a roof over your head and plenty of food. Hopefully he won't drink too much, but if he does, just stay clear of him. You'll manage. We always have." Mother's hands fell, defeated, to her sides. "It's faith in God that got me through my own marriage. I wish...."

I turned around. "What, Mother?"

"I wish you were able to find comfort in the Lord. I just think it would save you ever so much heartache. You feel too much. It's not good for a woman to feel too much."

I thought of the siren girls in the trees. The men and women forced to work on our own land. The black children sold away from their mothers. The fact that I was being traded from one man to an-other—my auction block the parlor. "There can be no God, Mother."

She put her hand to her heart. "Don't speak like that!"

"It's true. How can you stand there, in the life you have, and tell me God had anything to do with it? How can you look at Claudia and Annie and think this life is for the best? Are you blind? Or just blind enough?"

She slapped me so hard the hairpin she'd just replaced fell out of my hair. "Don't you dare speak to me that way. I have sacrificed for you! I have worked for you! I wanted you to have something better than I've had, and you have that chance with Jonathan. He's going to be in Congress one day. You'll have everything you need. Why isn't that enough for you? Ungrateful child! One day you'll have children of your own and you'll understand the way life works. It's not all about you! It is never all about you. We're here for others, Roberta. Not ourselves. The Lord wants us to serve. That's what women do."

"That's not what I do."

"Marriage will sure enough change that."

"Then I'll walk away."

"You don't get to walk away! Don't you see! What are you going to do? Start up your own plantation? What can a woman do but be a whore or a wife?"

"I'd rather be a whore."

She slapped me again, but as she walked out of the room, I knew by the slump of her shoulders she'd have rather been a whore than a wife as well. "You be presentable for Mr. du Bois!" she shouted from the stairs. "Your father has a lot riding on this."

I pressed my hand against my cheek. Through the open window, I heard the slaves singing. I didn't even begin to know how, with all their sufferings, they were able to pull anything out of their bodies that was even close to a song. When I walked among them I tried to be friendly. Most of the time they only mumbled to me. I needed them to like me in ways I don't think I understood. But how could they like me? And how could that make me feel any less guilty for the color of my skin and the size of my house? Nothing could do that. So I just brought them water, even though my father warned me not to, and they mumbled, "Thank you, Mistress," and continued with their work. The ones that dared make eye contact with me had the glare of stone. I began to be grateful when they simply drank the water and moved on.

When I was a little girl, living on my Daddy's cotton plantation in Chestney, South Carolina, I thought the world was only one way. I thought the coloreds worked for the white people everywhere. The whole world to me was those five hundred acres. Anything that reached beyond that was the stuff of fantasies. The stories I heard about the outside world were, I thought, as much the truth as the folk tales about Rumplestiltsken and Rip Van Winkle. My Daddy had a reputation for being one of the meanest of all the South Carolina plantation owners. He bought and sold with no regard for families. He taught me to think of the coloreds as groups of animals, like puppies, and thought nothing of separating the families like you would choose a dog from a litter. Mother and Daddy told me slaves had no souls. I never thought anything different until 1844 when my half-sister Claudia was born.

Claudia's mama, Annie, worked in the house for Mother. Mother hated Annie and she worked her ragged. Daddy used to sneak around at night "backwoodsin'" as they called it then. My Daddy loved backwoodsin' with Annie the best. When Claudia was born, her eyes were hazel, just like Daddy's, and Mother went into a rage.

"I want that woman out of my house! Send her to New Orleans! Send her to Florida, I don't care, but Thomas, so help me God, I want her gone or I'm going to kill her."

Something about that hazel-eyed baby got under Daddy's skin. He wouldn't separate Claudia from her mama. Since Mother knew he never gave any regard for family ties, this made her even madder. She threatened to beat Annie to death every time she dropped a dish. But Daddy wouldn't let her. And of course, that made Mother even more enraged.

Daddy took me to meet Claudia when she was about three. I was six then, and mostly kept to myself. I didn't have any brothers or sisters and at the time I didn't know why. Now, I imagine it was because Daddy was more interested in acquiring human property than human heirs. Or maybe Mother had just closed up. I understand more why a body would do that now.

"Look here, honey," Daddy said. "This here's your sister."

Annie wouldn't look at me as she gently pushed Claudia forward. The little girl moved on wobbly legs, like a baby goat. Her shoulders were wrapped in a yellow down blanket Daddy must have gotten from the big house. None of the other slave children had anything so nice and soft. It was almost as soft as the quilt on my own bed. I glanced at Daddy, who held his hands behind his back, beaming like he was showing off a prize hog. Claudia wobbled toward me, Annie's hands on her shoulders. Claudia reached for my hair, her tiny fingers uncurling, opening.

"My sister?" I looked at this girl and looked at Daddy and didn't remember Mother being big at all. Annie shuffled her feet.

"Claudia, this is Roberta," said Daddy.

"Berta." She giggled and hid behind Annie's skirts.

"Roberta, I want you to watch after Claudia. If anything happens to me, I want you to remember she's your sister." Daddy stroked his salt and pepper whiskers with his left hand. "Do you understand what I'm saying?"

I nodded, but I had no idea what he was talking about. Why wouldn't Claudia grow up like all the other Negro children and work in the fields or in the house? Why would Claudia be different? It had something to do with her hazel eyes and Mother's anger. That much I was old enough to understand. Daddy's hand lingered on Annie's pockmarked cheek. Annie visibly stiffened. Claudia held tighter to her mama's skirt. Annie whispered something in her ear, and she came closer to me.

"Miss 'Berta," she said, and glanced over her shoulder at Annie, who nodded her approval.

Those hazel eyes gazed up at my six-year-old self with awe. Claudia smiled, shyly at first, then wide, revealing a row of perfect tiny teeth. I had never seen Daddy behave like this. He looked at Annie so differently from the way he looked at Mother. He looked at Claudia so differently from the way he looked at me. I didn't know what to call it, but it sure was strong. Like his eyes were really open.

"Hello," I said. Claudia ran back behind Annie. Just the night before Daddy had been to town where he'd bought another fifty or so Negroes from one of the cargo boats. Even at six years old, I knew he didn't think of their families or their happiness. They were tools for his business. What did Annie have that the rest of the slaves didn't?

"Roberta, you remember, y'hear?" Daddy nodded at Annie who left the room with Claudia trailing behind her. "Things might happen one day. You don't ever know."

I've thought about those words for decades. Much later, in the spring of 1864, most of the plantations were left empty. The slaves took their chances on the roads and in the woods. The Yankees had come, and in that year, one year before the official end of the War, Daddy's slaves turned on him and hung him from a tree in the middle of the grounds. They burned the house to the earth and, legend goes, danced on the ashes. They burned the cotton fields too. Poured salt on the earth so nothing would grow for years. But that didn't matter. They were on the move. Times were changing and Daddy was hanging, bloated and blue, from a tree.

By the time that happened, I had already walked into Snaky Swamp. I watched from between the worlds. And if I could have reached through the sticky veil and helped him, I don't know that I would have. I wondered what flashed before his eyes as they dragged him through the same streets where he had dragged countless half-dead black bodies to their deaths. I wondered if he was capable of appreciating the irony of his own death. What could his last thoughts have been? Were they of Mother and me? Claudia and Annie? Or did he just die in a rage, like he lived?

I don't know where his spirit went. It doesn't walk the woods with me. It doesn't sit on the banks of the swamp and watch the alligators' eyes peek over the edge of the black water like stars. It doesn't blow cool air on the nape of my neck or sing with the osprey in the trees. I must admit I look for him at times. Times when Lillian and her daughter Hannah turn their backs on each other. Times when I feel I have almost approached the door to freedom, only to find it solid granite. That's when I look for my Daddy. Not the man who destroyed hundreds of lives. Not the man who broke Mother's heart. I just look for my Daddy, only he's nowhere at all.

Lillian Green
1951

The woman in the walls brought my voice back. Pulled it back, actually, from the place in my belly where it had been festering. I had stopped feeling like not speaking was unusual. In fact, my world became far less complicated once I no longer engaged with it. I went to school, listened to the radio, watched Truth or Consequences on our new black-and-white television set, and stared out my window. I no longer missed conversations. They never told the truth anyway. Even Mother and Daddy's conversations had constricted to baby snakes—one or two words followed by a hiss.

My window was open—the same window I'd climbed through that evening—and the swamp frogs chanted their hymns. There was no breeze to tickle me as I lay on the bed on top of my quilt. My tongue was suspended in between my upper and lower jaw. I moved it softly top to bottom, a dark sea anemone, its thick root at the base of my throat. The moon waxed, and I imagined it pregnant, about to birth a new light. Her moon-flesh would be pink as spring, soft but strong enough to push through hope. I rolled onto my side, pillow pressed against my abdomen, trying to capture the feeling of "pregnant," when the woman stepped out of the wall.

We'd been reading "The Yellow Wallpaper" in school and I was determined not to fall prey to the ghosts in that story. Walls simply didn't move. Not even in our haunted house. Sure, the drapes moved from time to time in unexpected ways, but as Mother always said whenever I mentioned anything strange, we lived in an old house and strange things just happened.

I closed my eyes. Opened them. She was there, not yellow, but pink. Her pink-feathered hat perched sideways on her head; her gown, pink velvet, wrapped around her feet like fingers. She was tall—much taller than Mother—and thin, as if breath itself would break her. She bent to kiss my forehead and I smelled the swamp— all the dead things and things that should be dead that lived there. I smelled mildew and wet flesh and the blood of the boy body Gabriel Wilson, and I screamed.

Mother opened the door without knocking and rushed to my bed. I screamed and screamed. I screamed so hard the screams caught one another and danced in my throat around the root of my tongue-anemone and made me cough. I screamed so hard my eyes poured water onto the quilt, onto the pillow of my imagined baby, onto the already wet and dripping woman in pink. My nose leaked and I pressed my forehead into Mother's shoulder, the first time I could remember that shoulder staying put, not pulling away. The swamp frogs sang a different song and a surprise summer breeze kissed the pink feather on the woman's hat.

"I know, honey," said Mother. "I know."

You do? No, no, Mother can't know. No, no.

"I know, baby," she said, her thin arms circling me. "Mother knows."

But Mother was already on the other side of the room searching for a handkerchief in my dresser drawer, and the arms around me were wet and bony, and the pink feather tickled my cheek and I inhaled her swamp and quieted, settling into what would become the rest of my life.

August 3, 1966

Dear Mommy,

I can't find you. I see other people in the house, but I can't find you. Are you with them in the walls?

I miss you. Where did you go? Please come find me. I'm going to write letters to you since you won't talk much to me. I'll leave them right on the kitchen table in a pile where the flowers go so you won't miss them.

Love,
Your Daughter Hannah Green
Age 8

Roberta du Bois

I saw Gabriel for the first time after I gave Lillian her voice back. The family, on a rare occasion, had gone out to meet one of Lillian's father's client's families for dinner. He had stopped bringing clients home after Tommy left, which meant one less thing Lillian's parents had to talk about. The colored man who used to take care of the yard went away. I don't know if he was fired, or if he just couldn't bring himself to come back. Lillian's father did some work on the yard on Saturdays, but mostly the grounds were left to their own preferences. Part of me wanted to see the roots and weeds take back the land and the house; part of me felt sorry for the house. It wasn't the house's fault so many things went so terribly wrong.

Gabriel appeared in front of me as if he'd been there all along. The darkness of his eyes frightened even me—imagine that! He reached a bent finger out to touch the snakebite on my neck. I saw the rope burns around his and knew at once this was part of how it had to be. He and I were in the walls together.

"Why did you want to die?" he asked me, his voice like melted fudge.

"It used to be clearer to me," I said. "But after all these years I've forgotten."

"What did it feel like for you?"

His torn muddy shirt clung to his back, one sleeve rent and dangling in front of him. The stains on the knees of his cotton trousers told part of the story of his last night. His shoulders were almost too big to fit within the walls. He could have crushed me with a hug.

"It felt out of order." I wasn't sure of the words. "It felt like there

was no one to meet me. Like I had come to a train station too early and had no choice but to wait until my family arrived."

He nodded. "Something was there for me, but it wasn't mine."

How could that be? "Whose was it?"

"Theirs. Tommy Green's. The rest of them."

"What are you supposed to do with it?" I was envious, partly, because he had been given something at all, even if it wasn't his own.

"Wait." He pulled out a pouch of loose tobacco, popped a wad in his mouth. He handed the pouch to me, but I waved it away. "Wait until I know." He spit the brown liquid between his teeth directly onto the inside of the wall. "What are you supposed to do?"

"Watch, I suppose. Just like I did when I was alive. Just watch with no power to do anything."

"What did you watch?"

What did I watch? What didn't I watch? Jonathan beating men as black as Gabriel until their white bones showed through. Babies picked like cotton bolls from mothers and sent to opposite ends of the great South. Ten and eleven-year-old girls big with white men's children. Me pressing Claudia's hand into scalding water. Me trying to please my mother, my father, my husband. Me hovering above myself when Jonathan took me. My father taking Annie out behind the big house. My father believing she wanted it. Me believing it too.

"I watched myself fade away. So much so it was easy to step into the water. Part of me thought I might even float, I had become so invisible and light."

"But you didn't float." He handed the tobacco pouch to me again. This time I took it and stuffed some in my mouth.

"I didn't float."

"I didn't fly."

We both spit our tobacco juice. The walls lurched sideways as the nicotine flooded me like swamp water.

"Nice to feel something, isn't it," he said.

Tobacco juice eased out my lips. I pressed the back of my hand to my mouth. "Sure is." I felt half in and half out of myself. For a moment, I thought if I swallowed the leaves, I'd find home. Home seemed so close, in the shifting walls, with my shifting stomach and suddenly throbbing neck.

"It's leaking out your bite there," he said.

My fingers touched the holes and then I touched them to my lips. Yes. Tobacco juice. "Thanks."

"What if this is all there is?" Gabriel wadded another lump in his mouth.

I felt like I could push right through the walls, through Lillian's window, down the tree she climbed the night she saw what she shouldn't have seen, over to the tree where Gabriel shouldn't have been, and back to Idyllic Grove of a hundred and seventeen years ago, where I might have the moment back when I could have killed my husband and changed everything. My wound cried for me.

Gabriel came closer. "Let me have that wound," he whispered, his tongue on my neck, lapping at the edges of the snakebite. "You can give it to me."

"What can you do with it?" I wanted to push him away. My wound was mine, not his, but his tongue, though swollen, was the warmest thing I'd felt in almost a century.

"I can turn it into something else."

I believed him and let him suck the poison from me. He finished and spit forcefully onto the floor between us.

"Step on it," he said.

It was thick under my boot, warm like an animal.

"What do you want it to be?" He was behind my eyes now and I saw his last moment. I saw him separate from the pain and hang a moment longer in the noose than necessary. I saw the blackness waiting for him over Tommy. It stretched its arms to him and Gabriel fell into them, sobbing.

"I want it to be Jonathan," I whispered.

Under my boot was Jonathan's head, springy like rubber. His

Carolina blue eyes stared at Gabriel, not me. I jumped and stomped, but Jonathan bounced right back, almost laughing. I stomped harder, harder, but his head kept growing until it exploded in front of me, dripping blue ink down the walls.

"That must not be what you really wanted it to be." Gabriel was back on his own side now, licking his fingers.

I want it to be me.

"I know."

"Know what? I didn't say anything."

"Didn't have to. I took your wound. Now I know."

He was gone then, along with the tobacco juice, the blue ink, and my breath. I touched my neck. The bite was still there, but it was dry. A scab had formed. I had to resist the urge to pick at it while I waited for Lillian to return. Now that she could speak, I had things to ask her. I reckoned Gabriel did too.

6
If a Tree Falls

Lillian Green
1957

I met Jay Transom at the grocer's when I was an old maid of twenty-two. He stood in line behind me and caught one of my cauliflowers that had fallen out of my shopping basket. His hazel eyes seemed not to blink, and when he asked me where I lived, I told him before I could remember not to.

The day of our first date, he drove up in his best friend's white Thunderbird, rolling up to my house like he was driving a chariot. Daddy sat on the porch, as was his ritual, looking at whoever came and went, a glass of untouched scotch in his right hand. Daddy didn't raise his gaze when Jay walked up the porch steps. I held out my hand to Jay, and he kissed it and I felt a tingling clear through to my feet, just like I'd read about in *Vogue*.

The kiss caused Daddy to look up, a dime-sized wad of wintergreen Skoal forming a bump in his left cheek.

"Daddy, this is Jay Transom."

"Evening, sir." Jay extended his hand. Daddy spit the tobacco on the porch board.

"Don't worry about him," I said. "Let's get going." I paused, realizing I was pushing, trying too hard, doing everything I'd read wasn't attractive to boys. "That is, if it's all right with you."

"Yes, ma'am," he said. "You look quite beautiful tonight."

I felt that clear to my toes too.

The white Thunderbird had white leather interior that smelled of new shoes. Jay's long dark brown hair was wavy, slicked back from his face a little too crisply. I knew Daddy would have a comment about that hair length when I got home. I leaned back against the seat, stretching my right arm out the window. I wore a sleeveless dress and my skin smelled of rose. He reached for my arm like he was touching a frightened kitten and began to drum his fingers lightly on my flesh. Ba-rum-rum-rum. Ba-ba-rum-rum-rum. I smiled, so he reached for my leg and now with both hands, tapped a rhythm on my body. He started to hum "The Battle Hymn of the Republic."

"You don't know any other songs, Mr. Transom?" I asked him, still smiling, still dangling my right arm out the car window. If he didn't start driving soon, he might not need to. "Maybe something a bit more contemporary?"

"I'm sure I do." He still kept both hands on my body. "But for the life of me, I can't remember any of them."

We went to the drive-in. The air was cool and damp. Crickets chirped. Mosquitoes buzzed. It was a little too muggy to be outdoors, but I didn't mind. Tiny beads of clear sweat popped along the base of my neck, dripping down into my dress, below my breasts, down to my belly. For the first time, I followed the sweat with my mind, trying to imagine the crevices and marks on my flesh along the way to my navel.

Later, he remembered a different song. "For Auld Lang Syne." Don't ask me why. But it became our song. When he was finished singing, I kissed him, not worried at all about being a harlot. One of the real kisses with the tongue and everything. When our lips separated, he pulled my hands down and held them close and we just breathed together. In—out. In—out.

We never went any farther than a kiss that first night at the drive-in. He was trying to be a gentleman, but it was me who wanted him to take me down. I was tired of waiting. Tired of reading. Tired of remembering. Tired of talking only to ghosts. It was me, all soft and rose-smelly, who wanted to lie in the backseat and count the stars through the open sunroof with his hands on my belly.

He told me some about Korea, but not very much. He had been

a sniper, and the way he said those words made me know I couldn't ask him any more about it.

I told him just a little about Tommy. "We visit him at Christmas and Easter. We bring him turkey."

"I'm sure he appreciates that."

"He doesn't know we come."

"How do you know?"

"Because he rocks. Back and forth. Just like a baby. Only he's not a baby. He's my big brother."

"I'll bet he knows you're there."

I felt my eyes turn cool. "You don't know anything."

"I'm sorry. You're right. I don't. I only meant that, you know, people sometimes have a sense about them. They know what's going on, even when you don't think they do."

"Like people in comas."

"Right. Like people in comas."

"Tommy's not in a coma. Tommy's crazy."

When I said the word "crazy," my jaw clamped down on the letters. The "z" tickled my throat. I closed my eyes, even though I knew shutting them, along with my sweat, would make my brown eyeliner smudge at the corners. I should have worn false eyelashes.

"Hey," he said. "Let's talk about something else."

"It's just that whenever I think about Tommy I get a little sad."

"Don't worry." He took my hand. "We can talk about whatever you want. Do whatever you want."

I smiled with my lips together, just like Mother. "My brother Tommy always brought me a peppermint stick. Every time he went to the store. No matter what."

"Maybe I can meet him."

I stiffened and slid closer to the door. "We don't ever bring anyone when we visit. It would confuse him."

"Of course."

I wanted to get back on track with touching instead of talking.

"Jay, what is it you do for a living now that you're back from Korea?"

"A little of this and a little of that."

"When a man does a little of this and a little of that, where might he go and do that?" I smiled and thought about sucking on a peppermint stick.

"Here and there." He reached for my hand again, and this time I let him hold it between his palms.

"Mr. Transom, you're quite the man of mystery."

"I don't know as I'd say that. I just don't really have what you'd call a steady job. I tried college, but it wasn't for me."

"Why not?"

The movie had started. The flickering from the images on the screen danced over our faces. Since we hadn't turned the speakers on, we couldn't hear the words, only the noises from the cars around us. Just our breathing.

"I don't know. Guess I can't see as I'd have much use for it."

"Education helps everybody, Mr. Transom."

"I imagine. But I'm not really everybody."

"No." I studied his hands. "I'd say you must be a farmer, but your hands are too soft."

"I'm not a farmer."

"I'd say maybe you work the tobacco auction, but your teeth are too white."

He put his finger to my lips. "You really want to know what I do for a living?"

I nodded.

"I sing, Miss Lillian Green. I sing in the clubs. I sing anywhere anyone will have me."

"You're a nightclub man?" The filmstrip ran through my mind of everything I was ever told about nightclub men. Danger. Beep. Stay away. Beep. Rapists. Beep. Freeloaders. Beep. I could almost hear Daddy's voice, "Darlin', you stay away from those nightclub men." And then of course, "especially the ones with the long hair."

"I didn't want to tell you. I wanted you to like me first." He fiddled with the keys that dangled from the ignition like limp collard greens.

I considered that for a moment. "What makes you think I don't like you now, Mr. Transom?"

"I don't know. Something about the way you pulled away from me. Something in your eyes."

"What do you see in my eyes now?"

"I—I don't know, Miss Green."

"I tell you what." I scooted closer to him on the sticky leather seats. "You take me to some of these nightclubs, show me what they're like, and I'll tell Daddy you're an accountant." I smiled; wicked.

He touched my open lips again with his index finger.

"What do you say, Mr. Transom? I've never seen a nightclub before."

On the movie screen, John Wayne held tight to his hat. Dust swirled around his legs. "You want to go tonight?"

"Could we?" I scooted even closer to him. I was entranced by my sweat, my slippery skin, my desire to slither. I didn't want to do anything to jeopardize this moment. This is the moment, I thought. I will always remember this moment.

"We could," he said, and turned the key. "You sure you're ready?"

"I've been waiting my whole life."

September 23, 1968

Dear Mommy,

I see more than one person in the house. I just saw someone's eyes, just eyes! Are other people's houses like this? I don't think so. I'm going to leave these letters around the house for you instead of just on the kitchen table. Maybe you'll find them and write back to me if I put them in more than one place.

Love,
Your Daughter Hannah
Age 10

Lillian Green
1957

Jay was what you'd have called a real ladies' man. He sort of eased himself into you, if you know what I mean. You'd be sitting out on the porch holding a half-full glass of tea, and before you could say spit you'd feel a touch on the back of your neck, light enough to be the wind. You'd turn around and there he'd be, grin big enough to eat you alive. You'd kiss him then, because it's all you could do. Kiss him. Hold him close to you. Wonder when he'd be gone.

It was just like that. I didn't know any better. My idea of true love was Mother and Daddy sitting on opposite ends of a long table, passing salt between them. I didn't know what to think when Jay came around. Mother liked him right away, but Daddy never did ease up on him. Daddy liked to tell me his instincts were never wrong. Said it to me a lot after Jay and I parted company.

Jay took me slowly that first night. Moved in and out of me like syrup. I thought my whole life I'd be the kind who'd wait until she was married. I didn't know the first thing about passion when I thought those thoughts. I didn't know a touch on the small of my back could turn my bones to Jell-O.

We lay on my bed, on top of the quilt that Mother and her fore-mothers had taken care to keep in good condition through four generations. Mother and Daddy were miles away in town at the church dinner-on-the-grounds. I rolled onto my belly, the wonder of cool air on my naked back fresh in my mouth, and opened my lips again.

It wasn't too long before I figured out that skin on skin told the best kind of lies, and the closer someone gets to your body, the easier it is for them to breathe in and out with you until you begin to forget how to breathe yourself. Jay would ask me more and more questions about Tommy, and I learned there were ways I could avoid answering him that I'd never considered before meeting him. It seemed all I had to do was smile and touch the back of his neck and I could change the subject to something that didn't pull at my throat.

I wanted to get as far away from Mother and Daddy and Tommy and that night in the woods as I possibly could. I wanted to make myself over into a sweet, simple Southern belle who drawled over carrot cake and homemade biscuits. I wanted to think about cotillions and the 1-2-3 1-2-3 of an old fashioned waltz. I thought Jay could be the way out for me, but I'm afraid I never quite mastered the recipe for carrot cake, and when I danced I always stepped on my partner's toes. Even when I danced alone in front of the mirror.

I had gotten pregnant, and 1957 was not the best time for that announcement. I had decided to tell Jay he had to leave, even though I knew it would break my heart. My secret about Tommy was even bigger than his secrets from Korea. Soon, everyone would know about the baby, and I couldn't be sure what Mother and Daddy would make me do. I didn't think Jay was the marrying kind.

The air was heavy, but not so heavy as to be oppressive. I just knew I was surrounded by something organic. Something safe. A hint of ocean salt made me wonder if a storm was moving in. I had to tell Jay about Tommy, and if it went well, then I could tell him about the baby. Maybe it could work out OK and we'd end up married like the couples in the newspaper. But I didn't really believe that. He'd have to go, once he knew the truth about what a terrible person I was. He couldn't want me to be the mother of his child.

Jay and I sat out on the porch in the swing. My legs folded over his, which were stretched out onto the patio table. His gray felt cap was pulled down to shade his eyes; a few wisps of curly hair poked out from beneath it. I held a glass of lemonade I'd squeezed that morning, the surface of the glass damp with sweat. We rocked a little, so slowly it was noticeable only by the creaking of the chains that held the swing suspended to the porch ceiling. I saw a brilliant cardinal fly in front of us. I thought Jay was asleep. This would give me the perfect opportunity to think of a way to begin the conversation. But then, much to my surprise, he spoke what I feared most.

"Aren't you ever going to tell me what's wrong with your brother?" He didn't look at me, just sort of looked under his hat brim, toward the creek.

Eenie meenie miney mo

I took a swallow of lemonade, lost my courage and lied. "Honey, I told you. Tommy went a little off when he was a boy. Doctors can't seem to do anything about it."

"That don't seem right. I mean, they can do so many things now. That electroshock stuff I read about in the paper. Seems to work wonders on people they thought before couldn't be helped. It's nothing to be ashamed of, Lily. He's just sick." Jay took my glass of lemonade and sipped. "Ain't that right? He's just sick."

"We are not going to zap Tommy like he's in the electric chair." I uncurled my legs and placed them straight out in front of me. "He's not a criminal."

"I didn't mean to say he was a criminal. It's treatment, Lillian. Scientific advances! Don't you want the best for your brother?"

Catch a nigger by the toe

A drop of sweat trickled down my spine, spreading out at the edge of my cotton underwear. My mouth felt fat. My nostrils flared and I thought for sure Jay would notice because they had to be flaring wide as a mule's, but he just kept rocking us back and forth, hat pushed down on his forehead, waiting for me to speak. I set the glass of lemonade on the floor. The cardinal was back, only this time with company. The less-brilliant female perched next to him on the porch railing.

"It's such a pretty day," I said, noticing the gray clouds gathering to the east. "What do we need to talk about such things for?"

Jay stopped rocking the swing, took his hat off and took my hand, which I hadn't noticed was shaking. "We need to talk about such things because you won't talk about such things. If we're going to have a future, I want to know all about you. Whatever it is. I love you, Lily. Why won't you trust me?"

Maybe because my hand had stopped shaking once he wrapped his own around it. Maybe because the pair of cardinals stood, still as statues. Maybe because I let myself believe, for a single moment, that he meant what he said. So I spoke. I told him about sneaking out of the house. About watching Tommy in the woods. About the boy, whose name I now knew to be Gabriel Wilson, swinging in the tree. I told him how I'd held this story inside for all these years. Tommy made himself go crazy. Tommy destroyed his own life. It wasn't me. I never told. I never told. I never told.

And as the words poured out of my mouth like dead fish I watched him moving farther and farther away from me. I watched him close up. He picked up his hat. The cardinals flew away. He released my hand and the trembling started again.

Jay stood up. He seemed so tall to me right then, so power-ful and beautiful. His eyes grew darker. The deep hazel color that blended so nicely with his tan skin was edged in black. It must be the shadow from his cap. It must be. He cleared his throat. The words still poured out of me. They had been captive so long. I couldn't stop now if I wanted to. I didn't want to. Not really. The release of the grip around my throat felt so wonderful.

I finished. My hands were still. My face was cold; wet. Where did he go? Why didn't he reach for me? I gave him my pain and he left it hanging between us. He had walked down the three steps to the yard, and stood, looking out at the creek, his back to me.

"Jay?"

My sandaled foot began to twitch. The glass of lemonade tipped over. The collie from across the creek barked. Maybe he saw cardinals of his own. When Jay turned back to me, his face was wet, too. Surely now, I thought. Surely now he'd embrace me. He'd recognize what a burden I have carried all these years. He'd understand I was just a girl. Just a baby girl of fourteen.

But none of that happened.

"Your brother killed Gabriel Wilson?" His voice was too steady, like Daddy's would get right before he exploded.

"You remember the lynching?" I was surprised.

"I remember."

"Yes, Jay. It was Tommy."

"And you saw the whole thing?"

If he hollers let him go.
Eenie, meenie, miney mo.

"I saw."

"You didn't say a word? Not to anyone? Not to Tommy? Not to your parents?"

I was crying, hard, and the words were guttural. "I loved my brother, Jay. Can't you understand? Say you understand!"

"Gabriel Wilson was my cousin."

My knees gave out and I reached behind me for the porch swing, which had long since stopped swinging. Jay reached in his pocket for his car keys and walked towards his car.

"Don't go! I don't understand! How is it possible–"

He spun around. "That you have been sleeping with a nigger? That you could have possibly expected redemption from me? That here it is 1957 and you still hated that man so much you couldn't even give his family some peace? Keeping that secret, Lillian, that tells me exactly who you are."

I heard his words, but they didn't seem to be true, or even possible. I was protecting my brother. Didn't that make sense too? "But you look so–"

"White. Yes. Well, you never know what you get sometimes when the blood gets all mixed up." He spit on the grass.

But he'd gone into restaurants with me. Drank from the same water fountains. "You've been pretending to be white?"

"I've been being what I have to be to survive. I fought for this country in Korea. I will not be told where I can eat." He wiped his cheek with the back of his hand. "Besides, I might be more white than you are. This area's so messed up in itself, nobody knows how all the blood flows, do they?"

I clutched my womb. My baby. My mouth opened and closed. An action I knew all too well. The silent opening and closing, like a fish on a hook, knowing the end is coming, but not sure how it came to be this way.

"Jay! I was only fourteen years old, and I–"

"You're not fourteen anymore, are you?"

This was it. I had spoken and in the speaking, lost everything. I lost everything by not speaking in 1949. Now I was losing it all again. I couldn't move. The hand on my throat held me back.

"I went fishing with Gabriel that day. He caught a huge catfish. He was so proud."

Jay left the yard, got into his car, and backed out of the winding driveway. I sat on the still swing, my toes sticky from the spilled lemonade, my hands shaking, my sobs silent.

"What did you have to go and tell that boy the truth for?" Mother asked. She was behind the screen door, feather duster in her left hand, right hand on her hip. "Not one bit of good can come from leaking that story out. We don't want folks all up in our business."

Jay had just driven away. My muscles had dissolved somehow during the conversation and I couldn't move.

"You hear me? He was a perfectly nice young man. A little too old, maybe, but it's not like you've got them crawling around up here."

I tried to will my hand to ball into a fist. I tried to will my arm to pull back and punch right through the screen door onto her self-righteous nose, but I couldn't move. Both my tongue and my body betrayed me.

"He was Gabriel's cousin, Mother." I hardly heard myself speak those words.

"What?" The screen was still between us.

"He was Gabriel's kin, Mother! Kin!"

"No need to shout at me," she said.

This time my body responded and I leapt from the porch swing and pushed both my hands through the screen. "You have let Tommy destroy every possibility for my life! You and Daddy pretending like he didn't kill someone! Pretending like he's the victim. Hiding out here like you're some persecuted prophet! Tommy killed someone. Not just someone. Gabriel Wilson. He had a family. A fish! He had life and Tommy took it. Tommy did! No one else! But it's me who's lost her life for it."

Mother recoiled against the sideboard in the entryway, knocking over a fake antique vase filled with fake hollyhocks. She dropped the feather duster.

"What's got into you, child?" Every word the same pitch.

I knew Daddy was in town. I could have done anything I wanted in that moment. Anything at all. All the words I'd stuffed into my womb began to unfurl and shoot out my mouth toward the sky. I imagined streamers of fire trailing after them as they launched.

Then I remembered my womb wasn't mine anymore and all I could do was clutch my belly and remember Jay's last touch and that I never told him I was pregnant and that there was nothing, really nothing, now that anyone could do. I sat back on the porch swing, all my flames extinguished. "I'm pregnant, Mother."

She picked up her feather duster. "Well, don't that explain it all, then."

We stared at each other through the torn screen door for a moment long enough to have connected us. But instead she said, "Your daddy's going to be upset about this door," and disappeared into the house.

October 17, 1968

Dear Ghost Woman in the Pink Feathered Hat,

Maybe if I leave letters for you you'll write back. I know I'm not crazy, no matter what the kids at school say. No matter what mama doesn't say. Maybe you could show her where I left the notes for her? Maybe you could tell her to read them? I think she talks to you. Maybe you could come talk to me?

I'm lonely here.

Your Friend,
Hannah Green
Age 10

Lillian Green
1957

I watched the storm clouds coming in from the east. The cardinals were gone. The spilled lemonade was a sticky puddle on the porch. I unbuckled my sandals and walked barefoot into the yard. Crushed pinecones, soft as felt, dotted the grass. Maybe it would rain after all. Crabgrass surrounded the flagstone path from the porch. I remembered when Daddy and Tommy laid the stones. It was an almost-rain day, like this day. Both Tommy and Daddy had taken their shirts off, although Mother always disapproved of that. I brought lemonade to them on a metal tray with prints of oranges on it. Daddy wiped his forehead with the back of his hand and squinted down at me when he took the glass.

"Thanks, punkin," he said.

Tommy, working behind Daddy, digging holes for the flagstones, winked at me. "Thanks, Butter Bean."

I didn't notice they both referred to me as vegetables. I just noticed they both referred to me with smiles.

Thunder rumbled. Unusual to have a storm this early in the day. I kept walking away from the house where the brown and gold curtains Mother made still billowed out in welcome to the visitors who no longer come. I walked until the ground became a nest of pine needles and damp leaves, the trees rising tall around me.

Eight years ago I walked through these same woods. Tinier feet crushing pinecones, some of which were probably still decaying beneath my current size nines. When I was little, I liked to dig up the earth out here in the woods, trying to uncover what lived on the very bottom. I think I was searching for a solid piece of concrete. Something that would signify to me that yes, indeed, I have reached the end. But of course, nothing like that existed.

The woods that surrounded my house were still full of unknowable bugs. Earthworms. Termites. Green iridescent beetles that curled into balls when they slept. Mosquitoes with silky legs and spiny bites. Snakes: Green ones, black ones, speckled ones, poison ones, good ones. I could even spot them from my bedroom window when I was little. Now, I practically have to step on them to know they're there.

Twigs snapped across my face from low-hanging branches. Thunder came again. I couldn't see any lightning, but I smelled the damp. The hot acidic smell of the creek, which of course was once a swamp in the glory days of the plantation, combined with the fresh water rain scent made me heady. Had I smelled the swamp on that night? Had I missed stepping on the head of a snake by one inch? Two? If I had been bitten by a cottonmouth, then I would never have seen. If I would have never seen, then I would have never kept the secret. If I had never kept the secret, Jay wouldn't be gone. Tommy wouldn't be gone. Maybe even Gabriel wouldn't be gone.

Rain fell slowly, but I barely felt it. The leaves on the trees held the drops. I heard it though, each drop the soft step of a fingertip drumming a tabletop. A chill traveled up from the earth through the soles of my feet. I wished for my shawl, but remembered that Jay was gone and thought it might be best if I leaned against a tree and froze to death. No one freezes to death in an Alderman spring, but the thought warmed me for some reason, and I almost laughed, even as I felt my ribs crack open and trace the arteries of my heart.

Eenie meenie miney mo
Catch a nigger by the toe
If he hollers let him go
Eenie meenie miney mo

Maybe it only made sense to me. Maybe loving my brother

wasn't a good enough reason. Gabriel had caught a catfish that night. Maybe his mama was going to fry it up for supper when he got back from wherever he was when Tommy and his friends caught him. I hadn't thought of that at all.

Jay was right to run. Who could stay with me? Certainly not someone like Jay. Someone who'd only been kind to me and to everyone I'd seen him with. I couldn't have expected him to understand. The layers a woman stretches across her soul are not penetrable by a man. I knew that even at twenty-two.

The rain fell harder, louder. I turned around and saw the house, my house, that had seen so much this day. It was a doll's house, really, a place for shells of people. If the rain kept up, Jay's tire tracks would be washed away and there would be nothing left at all except my sticky sandal and my trembling hands. And of course, our baby.

Daddy built the gray-blue wooden pier that stretched out over the creek. Tommy and I would toss nets over the side and catch crabs for supper. The sound of their pinchers struggling against the tin pails was nothing compared to the chorus of tiny screams from the pot of boiling water Mother tossed them into. I tried not to hear them because they tasted so good. Soft, tender, fleshy.

We'd fish off the end of the pier too. Once, I caught a boot, big, brown, with the sole flapping away like a toothless mouth. Tommy caught a rusted Tennessee license plate. We made up stories about how that could have come to be in the creek behind our house. Murder, we decided, and giggled. Someone murdered their best friend and sank the car in the Cape Fear River. Over a bag of gold! Tommy saved the plate. Kept it on his windowsill. I have it now, somewhere on a shelf in one of the closets.

The marsh grass along the edges of the creek stood as tall as I remembered Tommy. The black mud floor was filled with symmetrical holes for sand crabs. A pelican perched on one leg in the center of the grassland. I wondered if its beak was full of fish. I wondered why it wasn't trying to get out of the rain. My hair hung wet against the side of my face. Water ran off my ears, falling in loud drops to the ground.

Roberta du Bois

I went with Lillian to the hospital so she'd have someone look-ing out for her. Her mama was ashamed, unwed pregnant daughter and all that, and her daddy, well, her daddy was just about anywhere but there with either of those women. We may be born alone, we may die alone, and we may wander the earth alone, but it just doesn't seem right for a woman to give birth all alone.

I replaced the pitcher of water by her bedside with a pitcher of sweet tea. A woman needs her sugar. Dr. Wutherford had left her alone. He said she wasn't dilated enough yet. Needed another hour. The floor was short of nurses that night. Lillian didn't argue, but I could see the wiggling in her belly pushing right up against its first door.

Lillian struggled to stay on the small bed. The chrome bars held her in like a caged cat. The baby was coming. Didn't need to be a doctor to know that.

"I'm right here for you, honey," I whispered. I held my hands on her shoulders from behind, helping her ease into the mattress. "All you've got to do is breathe. She knows what to do."

She grabbed the bars and clamped her jaw.

"It's OK to make some noise, child."

But she couldn't. I saw the screams fall back down her esopha-gus to wrap around her liver and her spleen, joining hands around her spine. The jolt went through her body and the baby's head crowned. Dr. Wutherford was no doubt on the smoking porch.

"I got you, baby." I moved to the foot of the bed, crouched, and when I saw the crown, I almost lost my balance. Hair as red as delicious apples.

The moments between the baby's crowning and entering the world stretched like taffy. Lillian tried to hold her back, tried to stuff her back inside her, maybe to meet the screams, but the baby had her own will, and by the time her right foot was freed, Dr. Wutherford had returned, and of course, not seeing me, stepped right in front of me and caught the baby, slapped her bottom, and cut the cord as the baby screamed all the sounds her mother had never set free.

"Her name is Hannah," said Lillian as she swayed in the bed, hair clumped with sweat and fear. "Hannah. It's a name that's the same both ways."

Dr. Wutherford placed Hannah in her arms, muttered something about no nurses, and walked out, leaving mother, daughter and me as wide-eyed and breathless as if we'd just seen God. Hannah caught our breaths and expelled them back in shrieks that would have brought the walls of Jericho down. Lillian offered her breast, but Hannah refused it. It would be the last time Lillian offered freely, forging the labyrinth they both would walk the rest of their days.

June 12, 1969

Dear Mama,

I got out of bed last night and I saw you looking at the moon. I like the moon when it comes in through the window. It feels like God is watching.

I saw you were crying. Do you ever hear me cry? I used to cry a lot more than I do now. I'm getting grown up. I cry when I sing, though. Do any songs make you cry? Just about every song makes me cry. It's like when the notes move up my throat they shake everything loose and I can't help it. It's a good feeling though, like a spring rain.

What songs make you sad, Mama?

Love,
Your Daughter
Hannah
Age 11

Lillian Green
1961

When all is said and done it seems like nothing much is said and done. Nothing that matters for much, anyway. I told Jay everything I had in my heart to tell him. Been going on four years since I've seen him or heard from him. Was it so terrible? Did I really do something so terrible? I guess I couldn't really believe, for the little bit of time I lay in his arms, that a man like him could love me. And if you never let your heart believe it, then I guess you sure can count on it going away. This love thing is black magic, though, I swear on a stack of Bibles. I walk out on the front porch and I can smell the smoke from his Marlboro. I can feel the coolness of his breath on my neck when he pressed his tongue at that indention right inside the collarbone. I can re-imagine the shudder that strutted down my spine to my hipbones.

If he hated me, at least I'd know he thought of me. But he couldn't even bring himself to hate. He just shut me away. Is that what love does? That's what we did with Tommy, wasn't it? Shut him away up in Mecklenburg County? Shut him away from all of us. We couldn't talk about what he did. He couldn't talk about what he did. The sheriff didn't care about what he did. Who was left to be accountable? Only me. Didn't I hear Gabriel scream? Didn't I stand over his still-breathing body? Didn't I then walk away? At least Judas got thirty pieces of silver. What did I earn?

I think Tommy must be happier than any of us now, in a fog of psychotropic drugs, fed at the stroke of a clock, awakened by the groan of a vacuum cleaner outside his room. Memory may be one of the strongest poisons we have.

Our daughter Hannah is almost four years old now. She hasn't asked about her daddy too much yet, but I imagine it's only a matter of time. She has olive-toned skin that doesn't look like mine. Her hair is thick and curly, but it's a brilliant copper color that I've never seen before except in sunsets. It's so plain she comes from someplace else. I know the people talk. I'm too young, only twenty-six, but here I am already the crazy lady up in the house on the hill, trying to raise a daughter on her own.

Roberta du Bois

The first time I saw Hannah see me, she was playing with paper dolls on her bed. She was spread out across the quilt baby Faith had made, although I doubt she knew anything about Faith, or the significance of the material she was lying on. Even her mother didn't know. Though soon enough she'd find out.

She was humming an Aretha Franklin tune that afternoon. Lillian was in the kitchen making tuna fish casserole for supper. A warm breeze blew through the open window, tickling the back of Hannah's neck. She stopped humming. The arm of the paper doll fluttered. I made no rise in the wallpaper, but she saw me anyway and her mouth hung open. She was unafraid, curious. She reached her tiny arm to touch me and I reached back without thinking. I so wanted to connect.

When we touched, rather than pull away, she lingered, her flesh-and-blood fingers mingling into my energy. Rather than stop her before she took on too much, I let her experience the slight buzz of electricity that jolted through her body. I let her hover there, between the worlds, before I released her and she fell to the floor, more from surprise than from pain. She touched her fingers where they had been inside my arm and felt their tingle. She looked again at the place on the wall where she'd first seen me slide behind the velvet-edged wallpaper. I let my guard down, revealed a little more of myself to her. Let her see the pink-feathered hat. I covered up the snakebite on my neck. She stared, head tilted sideways, watching. Then, she spoke.

"I've seen you around here before."

"Yes."

"I see you in Mother's room a lot."

"Yes."

"Why?"

I had no answer for her.

She tried again. "Why?"

"Not everything in this world has a reason, child."

"You're lost."

The snakebite on my neck pulsed, the truth oozing drop by drop down my wounded throat. "In a way, perhaps."

She folded a blue dress over the shoulder of her paper doll. "You're either lost or you're not."

"That's what I used to think too."

"What's it like behind the wallpaper?"

"Sticky!"

She laughed. "How long are you going to live here?"

"As long as I have to."

"Will you know when to go?"

"I hope so."

"I hope so for me too." Hannah slid the pile of paper dolls and paper doll accessories into a shoebox. She twisted her mouth into a cork shape. "I'm thinking I should be going soon too."

"Where would you go?"

She shook her head. "I don't know. On the road. I want to go to Nashville."

"I think your mother would have something to say about that."

"Mama has nothing to say about anything."

"You know, grown-ups don't always have the answers."

"And ghosts do?"

Dear Mama,

Really, there are lots of people in the house. I think we should move. It can't be like this in other people's houses. Roberta's fun – she comes and talks and lets me draw pictures of her and touch the feather on her hat. But she isn't the only one who's here, you know. You do know, don't you?

There's a black man with a noose around his neck. He looks right through me and never ever talks to me. He dripped some blood on the carpet in my room, but I was able to clean it up before you saw it.

There's two black women too who hang around Roberta. They seem to want something from her. They make Roberta sad, which makes me sad. I want them to go away because they are making it hard to play with my friend. Sometimes I don't see her for weeks, and when I finally do, she tells me she's been visiting.

There's some other people here too, but I can't see anyone else clear enough to describe them to you, but I feel them. I feel the pulse of the whole house in my own heart. Don't you, Mama?

Love,
Hannah
Age 12

Hannah Green
1970

If you look high enough in the tops of the trees, you can see her. Anybody can. Mama sees her all the time, I know it. I see the way Mama drops a knife in the sink when she whisks by. I see the way she stares out the plate glass window, sometimes for hours at a time, when she thinks I'm not looking. I'm always looking. Just like she is.

I'm nine years old now and have never had anyone over to play. At school, everyone knows I live up at Idyllic Grove, which is enough to make them tease me for hours every day. I don't even care anymore. I can't do much of anything to stop it, so I just don't even try. I can play by myself just fine. And I'll tell you a secret. If I squint my eyes, I can see a lot of them moving around in our walls.

I should have paid more attention to what the other kids were saying about me. Then I would have known better. I might not have invited Roberta onto my bed to play cards with me. She might not have posed for me, in the window seat, while I tried to draw a picture of her in a pink-feathered hat. I might not have tried to take her to school for show and tell.

But I didn't know the biggest secret of all.

Once you give ghosts permission to come in, it's up to them to decide when to leave.

7
Shuttered

Hannah Green
1976

If the sins of the fathers are visited on the sons for seven generations, what, then, is the fate of the daughters? I am Hannah Green, daughter of Lillian, granddaughter of Gladys, great-granddaughter of Elizabeth, great-great-granddaughter of Faith, great-great-great-granddaughter of Claudia, great-great-great-great-granddaughter of Annie. I am the seventh generation. I am eighteen years old. In my veins I pump the world.

In 1958 I was born to Lillian and a man named Jay at New Hanover County Hospital. I didn't know Jay's last name. The story I heard tells it that Mama took one look at me and told the nurse I was her angel and that the heavens had opened up and given her my soul to keep her company all of her days. The nurse smiled sweetly and called the doctor, who gave Mama a Valium to help her "adjust" to motherhood. I'm sure if Mama had had her way, she'd have taken that Valium with a gin and tonic chaser, but hospitals being what they are, she had to settle for sweet tea from a plastic pitcher.

Mama has always been looking to be saved. Even the power of Christ is not enough for whatever Mama needs redemption from. She hoped I could save her, and when it became painfully obvious I could only try to save myself, she turned to silence, swallowing herself deeper with each inhale.

I only knew Jay from photographs. And there aren't many of those. He always stood slightly to the left in pictures, so his left arm is usually cut out of all the shots. He had wavy black hair almost to his shoulders, a bit long for the respectable gentleman. All the photographs are black and white, but Mama tells me his eyes were emerald green, like mine.

I know she thought they'd be together one way or the other, but they weren't. From the bits and pieces I can gather from Mama and Grandmother, there was a terrible fight—one of the types that in these days gets the police involved. But back then, nobody interfered in other people's business, and fighting could easily carry on all night. As long as there were no gunshots, people tended to stay out. The fight that night was one of the sort that went on for days and nights, stopping only to eat and sleep. Grandmother tells me Mama told him he had to leave. Mama tells me Grandmother has the story wrong, that there was no fighting at all, but she gives me nothing else. I like to think I have a memory of my father coming into my room and kissing my forehead while I was in the crib. I don't know if it's real or not, but it doesn't really matter. That moment of tenderness, whether it happened or not, helps hold my heart together.

I think it might have been easier for me to grow up without a father if Mama hadn't kept his spirit in the house. It was as if she caught it in a genie bottle and put it on the mantel so it could peer into everything we were doing. If it is true that Mama asked him to leave, I can't understand why she would want to keep him so close. She either never stopped loving him and wanted to keep his soul near her for comfort, or, she hated him so much she wanted to trap his soul so he couldn't love anyone else. Both are completely plausible, knowing Mama. I tend to lean toward the latter, except there are nights I can't sleep and I walk into the living room and she is sitting on the Victorian sofa staring at the black windows, tears falling as stars on her cheeks. Those nights I wonder if she could have loved him, and if so, what could have caused her to drive him away?

She talks in the middle of the night. She hardy speaks during the daylight, but at night, after she thinks I've gone to bed, she starts talking. It used to frighten me to listen to her carry on like that. Then, it grew to become a comfort. The sound of Mama's voice, no matter the occasion for it, soothed me. The rise and fall of her words as she argued and pleaded with the dark rocked me to sleep. I felt safe somehow, wrapped in the blanket of her nightmares.

In the mornings, she looked as perfectly put together as a Sunday school teacher, every hair lacquered in place, rouge shading her cheekbones, cranberry lipstick outlined with deep rose lip liner creating the perfect mouth. Only her eyes betrayed her nights. No matter how much mascara, how much waterproof liner and blended shadow, she couldn't create the illusion of brightness in her eyes. Every lash could be curled upward in a precise arc, but the blue eyes were dim; they reflected back what was in front of them; they never opened the window to what was behind them.

My grandmother has been dead for six years now. She lived across the creek, in a big old house that had been part of Idyllic Grove back before the Civil War. It had fallen to almost-ruin when the historical society stepped in and decided it could be a museum if we wanted it to be. Turned out, Mama wanted her mama out of this house more than she wanted to be left alone, so she let the contractors and the historical society people poke all around until the restoration was done. I thought when Grandmother moved out of the house, the ghosts might go with her, but I guess they weren't hers to take.

The house set back about a quarter mile from the road. We had to drive down a long dirt road past the two-man-tall cornfields to get to it. It was a two story, with a wide porch that circled the whole building. Rose bushes still grew wild in the front yard, twisting their thorny vines through the porch railings. In the kitchen was a wood stove courtesy of the historical society that Grandmother insisted on using to cook everything. In the winter, she used it to keep warm, even though the contractors had installed central heating and air conditioning. Mama couldn't understand what had happened to the woman who embraced the 1950s kitchen technology. She bought Grandmother a brand new electric range, and even went so far as to get her a TV so she might have something to do during the days she sat in front of the stove. As far as I know, she never even turned the TV on, and I know she never used the heat or the air conditioning. The place was always damp. Damp and hot or damp and cold. She liked it that way. The electric range "never cooked nothin' right," she said, and when she died it was clean enough to have been returned to the store, which suited the pearl-wearing historical society ladies just fine.

Mama never could figure out what happened to Grandmother once she went across the creek. Maybe she had her own ghosts after all. Seems like that's the kind of thing you never know for sure about a person.

That old place is empty now. Hal, the man who worked the field for us, got old too, and now stays pretty close to his home place. The field became a crop of weeds, sprinkled with the occasional wild tomato or cucumber. Beautiful wildflowers grow instead of the corn and the okra. Green snakes dart in and out around their stalks. The rose bushes almost reach the roof. Mama won't do anything about it.

People have been out talking to us about the house. People want to buy it, and they're offering a lot of money. We even had a movie studio ask about it. Mama isn't selling. She can see the old/new house from our porch, and she watches it fall into decay. She watches the land reclaim it, but she does nothing to stop it. All the new things inside will soon be swallowed by vines and molds and sand. Eventually, I suppose, if no one does anything, it will disappear into the landscape, swallowed up like Sleeping Beauty's kingdom. That seems to be what Mama wants anyway. I mentioned to her once about my moving out there and giving her some privacy since I'm eighteen now, but she wouldn't hear of it. She doesn't want anyone there. Not even her own daughter.

I can remember holidays at the big house right after Grandmother moved over there. Every window was lit brightly. The house blinked each time the door opened and another soul came or went.

Family I had never met before circled the porch, a glass of sherry or eggnog in their hands, heads tilted back, laughing. Mama and Grandmother worked in the kitchen together, peacefully for the only two times a year, at Christmas and Thanksgiving, dishing out sweet potatoes by the platter full, each one adding one more "secret ingredient" to the stuffing when the other had her back turned.

I was usually left to my own devices at these events. After I quickly demonstrated my ineptitude in the kitchen, Mama let me roam the house. Second and third cousins lounged on the circular staircase, catching up. The "old folks" sat straight in the high-backed dining room chairs, saucers resting on their knees, watching. I didn't know most of the people who appeared every Thanksgiving and Christmas day for turkey or ham. Mama and Grandmother led such reclusive lives the other three hundred and sixty-three days; I always marveled how they could arrange for twenty-five people to show up for the two major holidays at a place where I was certain they were strangers. But Mama and Grandmother knew them all, and they, carrying cloth covered pies and pitchers of sweet tea, knew Mama and Grandmother, kissed each one on the cheek, rubbing their lipstick prints away with index fingers. Mama and Grandmother seemed to like all of them too. Only after everyone had gone and the house was strewn with paper napkins, crystal goblets, and dropped forks, did the comments begin.

"Did you see Lena's hair color?"

"That color red looked like sheep's blood!"

"What about Arthur? Who was that hussy he brought?"

"Did you spend any time with Celia? Poor girl. Her daughter. Arrested!"

"Never mind about that! Suzannah's girl's pregnant. Joan says she won't say who the father is!"

"Bet it's Uncle George."

"Bite your tongue!"

And so it would go on, while we cleared the table and cleaned the stacks and stacks of dishes. I was big enough to help then but small enough to be talked in front of. I learned early on if you keep quiet and just dry the dishes, you could learn a whole world of information. Especially if it was on one of the only two nights a year the women in my life spoke in daylight.

Grandmother died when I was twelve. I was working in the vegetable garden at her house. She'd promised me five dollars if I pulled all the weeds from the okra. Mama'd come over to bring Grandmother's laundry. I'd just taken a lemonade break and was kneeling in the sand when Mama walked onto the back porch and let the screen door slam behind her. She held a peach-colored dishrag in her left hand. Her right hand flailed a bit around her head as her mouth opened and closed. I sat back on my heels, shielding my eyes from the sun with a gloved hand.

"Mama?"

She let her right hand fall to her side, leaned against the rail and released a sound like the chirp of a baby robin and shook her head.

"Mama? Are you OK?"

Her hand gripped the rail. She steadied herself and looked over her shoulder, toward the creek. "Mother's dead," she said, and turned and entered the house.

My first thought was whether she meant Grandmother or herself. Mama often talked about herself in the third person. I of course soon realized she meant her mother, but for a moment it made complete sense she would come to tell me that she, herself, had died. I waited, still kneeling in the sand, to feel something change. My throat did not constrict. My eyes did not water. My bones did not feel shaky.

I stood up and brushed the dirt off my jeans. When I went inside the house, Mama was playing the piano. The baby grand had been in the family longer than Mama and it desperately needed tuning from sitting uncared for in the damp house. She sat on the cushioned bench, wrists held high above the keys, as she, like I, had

been taught by Mrs. Creighton, the church organist. She was playing Rock of Ages, swaying left and right like she was in the choir.

"Mother always said I couldn't play," she said.

I pulled a chair from the dining room and sat next to her. Her
fingers stumbled over the keys. I began to hum.

She pumped the pedal. "Rock of Ages cleft for me—"

I joined in. "Let me hide myself in thee."

She stopped suddenly, lifted her hands and brought them down
to her lap. Her blue eyes welled, but she blinked quickly and pushed
the tears back down. "She always said I couldn't play," she whispered,
and closed the cover over the keys. I reached for her hands, but she
had already balled them into fists, rigid spheres at the ends of her
arms. "I guess I better call Pastor. We need to get things in order."

When Mama stood, the hem of her dress caught in the piano
bench. She tugged at it in short, powerful motions. She pried it free
and fell against the wall behind her. "Just like Mother," she said.

"What?"

"Catching me when I try to play." She shook her head and left
the room.

I sat in the dining room staring at the closed mouth of the piano,
trying to think of the perfect question I could ask Mama that would
open just the tiniest bit of her to me. I opened the cover and brushed
my fingers over the yellowing keys. "Rock of ages cleft for me..."

Mama slammed a door to an upstairs room. My fingers relaxed and my wrists rested on the keys. Grandmother didn't want
Mama to play piano. Mama never wanted me to sing. I should be
the grown-up and be in charge now. I should tell Mama I'd call Pastor and start making the arrangements. I should call the attorney
and use my biggest-girl voice. Instead, I sat on the piano bench and
watched the flat creek through the side screen door. Grandmother
had told a story once about alligators that lived in the creek, back
years and years ago. Once, to scare me and keep me from playing too
close to the edge of the pier, she even told me about a woman who

drowned in the water back when there was a plantation here. They said she wore a pink-feathered hat. It kept me away from the edge of the pier, but I was more concerned about the alligators than a dead body. Besides, I knew the woman with the pink-feathered hat was safe inside our house.

Lillian Green
1970

The morning Mother died, we'd had another of our silent conversations over tea and jelly biscuits. I watched her sit in that tiny front room, unmoving, although she had a whole house she could have wandered around in. That silent sitting broke my heart, though I had no idea how to talk to her about it. No idea how to reach her in her silence. She remained silent so long after everyone who could hurt her, except for Tommy, I suppose, was long gone. Maybe Mother had confided in him all the things it took me these past twenty-five years to uncover. Maybe she shut us all out because she had no choice. I'll never know now. I searched the attic for letters wrapped in rotted rubber bands that might tell me some of her secrets. But of course, I found nothing.

But I did find Mother. I had to get right up close to her to even know for certain that she had gone. For so many months she'd sat virtually unmoving in the orange La-Z-boy chair we'd had since Daddy died. I'd have to shake her to get any kind of reaction at all. She watched the electric stove like she used to watch the wood burning one we had back before Tommy went away. She never turned the stove on, just watched it, as if the burners would suddenly begin to glow on their own and catch the room on fire. She was always so much more afraid of electricity than real fire, even though she pretended to be Betty Crocker. Didn't trust any heat source that lived behind a switch, she told me once, when she thought I couldn't hear.

I always visited Mother in the morning and late afternoon. Late afternoons were my favorite time of the day. Made me remember afternoons decades ago when I'd come home from school and smell meatloaf cooking or maybe homemade yellow cake. Every afternoon long about four o'clock, a piece of sadness still hits me. I can't shake it, no matter where I am.

When I walked into the house, I should have known right away something was different. I heard too many noises. Usually when I walked into Mother's house I heard nothing. Not even the ticking from the grandfather clock in the hallway. But that afternoon the clock was chiming. Four o'clock on the nose. The house settled after the clock stopped, each creak from the wood sounding like woodpeckers hammering secret messages. Through the slanted sunlight from the long window at the top of the staircase, layers of dust floated down the stairs, dancing on their way to settle on the banister. I thought of Mary Poppins, light as wind, umbrella in hand, sailing down staircases in happy homes.

I carried a brown bag of fried chicken with me along with her laundry I did for her every two weeks. On Mondays, I always brought Mother a bag of chicken from the Sunday church potlucks. Chicken was her favorite part of the Sunday dinners, even though it was pretty much the one thing she never could cook very well. She used to go around and gather samplings from other women's fried chicken plates and take them home, eat them all, and then try again to figure out how to fry her own bird so it tasted even a tiny bit like anyone else's. She liked Amy Richardson's best, but Amy Richardson would have preferred to send her own flesh and blood to the devil than to tell Mother how she made her chicken.

I'd feel sad, watching her in the kitchen, burning batch after batch of perfectly good chicken, especially after Tommy went away. The chicken-cooking took on the intensity and urgency of guerilla warfare. Mother was obsessed. One Saturday, I came home from piano lessons and she was crying without any tears at the kitchen table. Her thin arms were folded "v's"; her hands covered her face and her arched body shook in tiny shudders like the movement of the cherry tree branches in a breeze.

"Mother, what's wrong?" I asked her. Her red-rimmed eyes blinked, confused, as if she were trying to place me in her life. "Mother, it's me, Lillian."

"Go," she whispered, covering her face with her hands again. I saw the burned dish of chicken on the stove. The charred skin bubbled. I backed out of the kitchen; hoping all the while she'd just look up at me once, acknowledge me once. But it didn't happen. She didn't. Or couldn't.

My bag of chicken had circular grease stains on it. I shouldn't have let it sit in the car for so long. I placed it on the counter by the kitchen door. Mother was wrapped in her gray shawl, the same shawl she'd worn ever since Daddy died. She was in front of the turned-off electric stove as if she could keep warm by the black burners. Her head hung a little to the right. I thought she was sleeping.

"Mother?"

She didn't move. Not so much as a shudder.

"Mother?"

The ticking from the grandfather clock synchronized with my own heartbeat. Goosebumps dotted my arms. I heard footsteps upstairs. Who's here? Mother! Is someone else here? Are you all right? I shook her shoulders and her head rolled back on her neck, mouth and eyes open. She was gone. I panicked. No blood. Who was upstairs? Was she murdered? Her flesh was too cold. I heard the clicking of low heels on the wooden floors. Mother's pumps. I raced up the staircase, clutching the banister with my hand, still greasy from the chicken bag. Mother will be angry if I leave hand-prints on the banister. Clack – clack – clack. The small diamond-shaped window at the top of the stairs was open, just slightly, and the air around it was cool. Mother! Clack – clack – clack. The odor of roses, sweet and strong, swept into the room. Mother always kept roses on her bedside table. Even out of season, she managed to find them at the florist. It was one of the few things she spent money on.

The aroma vanished as quickly as it appeared. The sound of clicking heels on the floors gone. The open window a gaping hole to the outside world. I touched the sill, my fingers leaving prints in the dust. I remembered her body, alone in the kitchen in front of a cold stove. Mother! Back down the stairs, greasy palms still streaking the banister. Clack – clack – clack. My own heels on the steps. No more mother. No more mother.

She was just where I'd left her. When I re-entered the kitchen, I didn't know exactly what to do next. I wrapped the gray shawl tighter around her. I took her aquamarine engagement ring off her finger and slipped it on my own. I looked for the phone, but remembered she had it disconnected. In the last few years, she thought people were spying on her through the phone line. I'd let her cut the service because I visited every day. I thought the real reason was she didn't want to spend the money each month just to talk to sales people. I never took the time to find out if she really was afraid of people spying on her. My mother. Did I know one thing about her that was real?

Strange, strange thoughts to be having. This is the day my mother died. Today. This day. Forever this day will be marked for me. Why don't I feel? Worried about spies in the telephone wires. Worried her dead body will get even colder. Worried the chicken will spoil. Chicken. Have to put the chicken in the refrigerator. Mother.

Mommy.

Nothing in the refrigerator but a pitcher of iced tea and some butter. Did you make this bag of chicken last a week? Mother. Were you hungry?

Hannah. Must go tell Hannah. She can help me figure out what to do. She's a resourceful girl. I closed the refrigerator door and left the house. Left my mother sitting in a rocker in front of a useless stove. She can never tell me about how Tommy changed her life. I can never tell her about how Tommy changed my life. All the time for telling is past. Nothing in front of us but swallowed vowels.

I found Hannah working in the garden. Her hair was pulled back in a ponytail and wrapped with a blue bandana. Sweat streaked her skin. She looked so beautiful to me. I opened my mouth and was going to tell her so, but the time for telling my daughter those things had also passed.

"Mother's dead," I said.

She stopped digging and looked at me, shielding her eyes from the sun with a gloved hand.

"What?" she said.

"Mother's dead." I steadied myself against the splintering porch railing and turned and entered the house.

The room spun. Clack – clack – clack. More heels on wooden floors. Who's here? No one is here! Go away! Go! Slam! The screen door behind me.

"Mama?"

Hannah! Go away!

"Mama, sit down."

Hannah! Can't you see? Can't you hear? She's here! She's here!

"Mama, sit down."

Mother! GO AWAY!

Clack – clack – clack.

"Mama, let me bring you some water."

"I don't need any water. Just go."

Whisper of roses on my neck.

"Mama, you look pale."

"Hannah, leave me."

My daughter, all of a sudden taller than I, holding a small glass of clear water, was the most beautiful creature I had ever seen. Did Mother ever look at me that way? Did she ever stop in the doorway to my bedroom and watch me sleep? Did she ever think, even for a moment, I was the most beautiful creature she'd ever seen? Maybe the same demons kept her tongue still as mine. My daughter set the

glass of water on the piano bench and went to the front porch. The
screen door slammed.

Roses. Thorns. Click – click – click. Dead blue eyes. Did she
speak last words? Did she think last thoughts? Maybe she only
fell asleep, closed her eyes for "a little rest" as she'd say, when Death
snatched her. Or maybe she was surprised, and shuddered, grasping
to hold on to that final breath.

Hannah Green
1976

I was nine years old, standing on my bed, singing "Respect" at the top of my lungs into one end of a jump rope. Mama was down the hall folding sheets into tiny squares. I heard her drop the laundry basket and run toward my room. My door was halfway open and I could see her, chest rising and falling, hand clutching her throat. I thought she was having a heart attack.

"Mama!" I jumped off the bed and ran to her.

"I'm fine, I'm fine," she said, holding me at arm's length. "What are you doing?"

"Singing."

"I can tell that."

"I was trying to sing like on the radio." I jumped back on the bed and pressed the plastic yellow jump rope handle to my lips.

Mama once again reached for her throat. "Where did you hear that song?"

"I told you. On the radio."

"A little girl. You're a little girl," she whispered.

"It's Aretha Franklin!"

"I know."

I was eleven the Sunday morning I gave a solo performance in church of "I'll Fly Away." I wore my black cotton robe with the wide white collar, and when Mrs. Eugene Wilson, the choir director, beckoned me forward with her heavy arms, I knew the most important moment of my short life was just about to arrive. I emerged from the mass of black robes to stand at the edge of the steps leading down from the choir loft. Mrs. Wilson nodded at me and the organ music surged like the tides.

Some glad mornin', when this life is o'er
I'll fly away

As my voice filled the church, Mama's lips parted slowly, her tongue tip slipping over her lower teeth. She adjusted the bobby pins on her black hat. She pressed her hand to her throat and stroked her skin like the neck of a kitten. The people sitting next to her shifted away from her, looking through their wire-rimmed glasses over the edges of their bulletins, wrinkling their noses. Mama kept her head facing forward.

I'll fly away old Glory, I'll fly away
To a land where gospel never ends
I'll fly away

I clapped my hands and shook my straight white girl-hips and eventually even the women sitting next to Mama trembled just a bit with the spirit. The choir behind me froze, mid-sway, and listened.

A-the mornin' when, the mornin' when

Pastor Thomas held his clear plastic cup of water in his right hand. The water sloshed from side to side. He kept his gaze on me—my small hands gliding through the air; my hair, pumpkin-orange, pulled back in a pony tail tied with a white organza ribbon; my feet, tapping the beat in black patent leather shoes and white lace socks. I finished the song, stretching the final word away out as long as I could into a string of half steps that climbed the scale. I exhaled, too loudly I thought, and looked at the congregation, my skin beaded with sweat, my throat tingling from the sounds.

Nobody moved. Not Pastor Thomas. Not Mama. Not the proper ladies sitting next to her. Not Mrs. Eugene Wilson. Not the choir behind me. Adrenaline surged and I needed a release. My tongue danced on the roof of my mouth.

Old Mrs. Phillips stood up from the amen pew. "That girl sings like a colored girl!"

Mama closed her eyes. Mrs. Wilson spun around to see who had spoken up. Pastor Thomas set his glass of water on the pulpit. Mrs. Phillips fanned herself with the bulletin, her lips twitching like a fly caught in web. My tongue stopped dancing and fell limp into the pit of my mouth. Someone shushed someone who shushed someone else. Everyone looked at me.

"Well, she does!"

I wasn't even sure I knew what it meant to sing like a colored girl, but I could tell by the silence of the voices and the loudness of the fidgeting that it was something terrible. I ran past Mrs. Wilson, over the kneeling bench, to Mama, who sat, back rigid, gloved hands crossed on her lap. I leaned my head against her shoulder, but it felt cold and hard to me. Her arms did not open.

Pastor Thomas cleared his throat. "Thank you, Hannah, for honoring us with your song."

Mama tapped my leg. "Come on. We're leaving."

I grabbed my sweater from the floor. "I have to take off my robe," I whispered.

"We'll bring it back later."

Mama picked up her black Sunday purse from the pew, took my hand, and marched us both straight down the aisle and out the front door. We kept walking. Past the cemetery under the willow trees where four generations of our family rested. Past Pastor's green Impala, parked crooked as always. Past the nursery kids who were playing in the sand by the side of the road. When we made it to our car, she opened the passenger door and pushed me inside without a word. She started the engine, and never once looking at me, backed out of the parking lot and headed home.

I felt all mixed up inside. Part of me was still bursting with the excitement of my first public performance, but that joy was quickly being overtaken by a shame I didn't know what to do with. Could a person sing wrong? Maybe I was flat. Maybe I was too loud and it just wasn't proper for church.

We stopped at the light next to the Piggly Wiggly. While Mama waited for the light to turn green, she drummed her fingers on the steering wheel. I knew better than to talk. The light changed. She turned her head left, then right, then proceeded into the intersection, the last one before the turnoff into our driveway. Mama parked under the same grouping of five pine trees she'd parked under all of my life. We sat in the car, the tick-tick of the cooling engine the only thing I could hear except my breath.

"Hannah," said Mama, "you're never to sing like that again." She pulled the keys out of the ignition, took her black pocketbook, and left me in the car.

I opened my mouth. The sound at the back of my throat felt alive—a creature trying to crawl over my tongue and through the double doors of my lips. It crackled.

"Some glad mornin' ...." I started slow, hoping to ease the voice out from behind its barricade. It was soft, noncommittal. "I'll fly away." It whispered, puttered, fell quiet. The ticking of the engine stopped. I thought I saw a pair of brown eyes laughing from the clouds. The pine branches danced above the roof of the car, celebrating the silence of the wind.

Lillian Green
1970

My mother's house without my mother was filled with stories. In every room, I saw conversations we never had unfolding like paper dolls. The paper sack of fried chicken I'd brought still sat in the center of the table. Flies would find it soon. The undertakers had carried her off with dignity—those young boys who thought death was still reserved for other folks touched her as they would antiquity. One of them even spoke to me.

"She sure lived a long time, ma'am," he said, his red freckles dancing through the prism of my tears.

"She sure did," I said.

And they left with her and her favorite navy blue suit she'd wanted to be buried in. They didn't wait long enough once they got out the front door to speak.

"She didn't look like a witch," one of them said.

"No, just weird," said the other.

"I always wondered what was back up in here."

"When I was a kid, we thought it was haunted."

They laughed then, and put my mother in the back of the spit-polished hearse and drove away.

I wandered upstairs to the place I'd smelled the roses.

Nothing.

I opened her bedroom door. The four-poster mahogany bed was made smooth, hospital corners visible under the thin crochet coverlet. Powder and a powder puff sat on the nightstand. She had been reading *The Lion, the Witch, and the Wardrobe*. I pulled open the heavy royal blue drapes and released a cloud of dust and spiders. The window was stuck shut. I wanted to break the glass to let in some air, but something stopped my arm.

I turned back to her bed and saw how it could have been. Me, sitting on the edge of the bed, knees together like a lady. Mother in bed, too light now to even make an indention in the feather pillow under her head. I'd hold her hand and she'd open her eyes, so glad to see me. I'd kiss the back of her hand, smooth her hair, as if we'd been this familiar our entire lives. I'd help her pass, letting her know she was loved and understood, and she'd help me pass by doing the same. After decades of silences, words would flow between us like breath. I'd catch her exhales in my mouth and send them back to her, dancing across the space between us. I'd put her red lipstick on her lips, so she could meet her Maker proper. And as I watched the woman who brought me here move on, I'd cry real tears of loss for something tangible, instead of these saltier tears of lack and self-pity.

But nothing.

In the kitchen, we were eating the chicken straight from the paper sack and she said thank you for bringing it and told me how much she wished things had been different. She refilled my iced tea and offered cornbread. She told me it wasn't my fault Tommy went crazy. She told me she should have seen the signs sooner. She told me I was just a little girl. She told me she used the electric stove when I wasn't watching. She just wanted to make me think she didn't. And we smiled at each other, lips shiny with grease, and clinked our glasses together.

But nothing.

In the parlor, the velvet cushions hadn't been cleaned in years, but we still sat on them and drank tea in white china cups, two lumps of sugar apiece. We gossiped about the latest scandal in the city council and laughed like schoolgirls. She placed her teacup in its saucer and moved to the piano, where with great flair and flounce, she proceeded to bounce into one of Scott Joplin's rags. She threw her head back and shrieked as her hands took on lives of their own up and down the ivories. I put my own teacup in its saucer and began to dance on the dark, thin carpet, my feet no longer my own, responding to my mother's hands, trusting those hands would guide my feet safely wherever they wanted to go.

Nothing.

Nothing.

My feet didn't know how to move. They have never known how to move.

Mother, I'd have danced for you. I would have surely danced to beat the day.

8
The Barter System

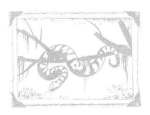

Roberta du Bois

When I was a little girl, the woods were full of magic. That was something you learned early if you were going to survive. Mother liked to pretend like she was a Christian and go to the meeting house every week, but she still poured salt in front of the door and she still cleaned every stray hair from her brush at night and burned them in the fireplace. Mother could tell me till she was blue in the face there was no such thing as ghosts, but I saw them. Not just me, but other people saw them too. And I know Mother did, else she wouldn't have woken up in a panic in the middle of the night when she forgot to clean her brush. She acted far too certain those ghosts weren't there to truly believe it.

Our slaves called them "haints." They knew what was living in the woods. They knew what was swimming in the swamp. Some were afraid of them. Others, like Lorita, were drawn to them. Lorita lived off the main road a little bit apart from most of the other slave shacks. She was a powerful woman. People came to her when they had no place else to go. Even we white people came to her every once in awhile when our white god couldn't help.

Lorita lived alone. Her house was on the outskirts of the plantation village, but from her doorway, she could see the fires in the woods where the slaves went dancing in the dark. She never had to join them. They always came to her. Lorita's shack was tidy. A small altar that could hastily be covered up or mistaken for clutter if the overseer stumbled by decorated the north corner. A dried cow's tongue was tacked above the door.

At almost six feet tall, Lorita was one of the biggest women on the plantation. She was one of the strongest too. Her hair was thick and curled tight. She wore a red scarf around her head, her hair streaming out from the back of it like a tail. Her skin was the color of burnt cherry wood, her nose wide and flat. Her cheeks were scarred with four cuts. No one ever asked and Lorita never said where they came from. Her hands were huge, even for a woman her size, and the skin had calluses the shapes of question marks. Still, she kept long solid fingernails, an inch long, and wore a red gris-gris around her neck. Her back was a collage of scars. At her throat, a jagged scar that in candlelight made her look like she had two mouths. Most of her teeth were gone, but when she smiled she had the warmest eyes of anyone around.

Lorita had been living on our plantation for twenty-three years. She was born on a sugar plantation down out of New Orleans to a mama who had just walked off the slave ship into bondage. She never knew her daddy, but her mama told her he was a powerful African King. Her mama was a Yoruban priestess. Since it was illegal to practice any of the African religions, her mama had gone underground. Folks knew her by sight. By smell. When her mama was finally caught, Lorita had watched from behind a tree while they burned her alive on a pyre. Her mama jumped and screamed and cursed and Lorita saw her change shape into a snake and all the white people fell to the ground shouting Hail Mary. Through the flames, Lorita saw her mama become nothing but eyes, then fall away. The white people couldn't touch the pyre for weeks. The heat from the flames never cooled. Lorita ran as far as she could run, but she hit swamp and alligators and snakes and panicked, was captured and returned to the sugar plantation.

She never made that mistake again. Lorita was untouchable. After the blood dried black on her back, even the old master from the sugar plantation left her alone. There was something in Lorita's eyes that made the white men quiver. That same something made the black women smile. When she was thirty-two, she was sold to my husband's daddy, who had hoped she'd bring many children. He liked the ample flesh of the large woman, and anticipated bending her over behind a shack, but Lorita turned her eyes on him the first time he approached her on Market Street and he backed away, tossing coins at the overseer, barking an order to "watch" her.

Lorita knew all about the hauntings in the woods. She knew about the four spirits that visited me. She knew the way they sang to me, the way their hair wrapped around the columns on the front porch and made them hang there, limp as rag dolls, waiting for me to sing back to them. They wanted me to think they were dead. They wanted me to get close enough to them so they could stretch out their transparent arms and catch me and drag me into the swamp with them. They waited for me. They had followed me from my daddy's house to my husband's house. No matter where I slept, they were there, dancing on the ceiling in my dreams.

The first time I talked to Lorita about them, she turned her eyes on me and I almost froze, my words falling letter by letter back down my throat.

"You bit?" she asked me, stroking the scar on her throat.

"Pardon me?"

"Your spirit. You bit?" She crouched low, her back to me, stirring something in a black pot over the fire. "I know you is. That be about the only reason the white folks come visitin' Lorita." She stood and turned back to look at me. I leaned against the doorframe, my bones feeling more brittle than the wood. "You ain't big. I can tell that just by lookin' at you."

I shook my head. "I'm not pregnant." Of course she might think that. It was the most likely reason a white woman would come visit her.

She walked the two steps it took to stand directly in front of me. She was at least ten inches taller than I. The width of her torso astonished me. No wonder Jonathan stayed clear of her. What was I doing here? I could probably creep away back to my polished, dust-free bedroom and no one would be the wiser. Her eyes were the brown of Snaky Swamp. The right one had specs of black around the pupil. She touched my cheek with her enormous hand. Her palm was rough as rock, but tender. The roundness of my cheek against the flatness of her palm struck me as natural. My pale flesh in her pink-black palm felt right. My gaze met hers, and I turned from her, knowing without knowing that with the briefest of glances she had seen a part of me that lived only in the patches of time between darkness and dawn.

"What they look like?" she said, never removing her hand from my cheek.

"There are four of them." I spoke almost involuntarily, as if Lorita were pulling the words from my mouth with fishing line. "They dance."

"How?"

"What do you mean?"

"How they dance? In a line or in a circle?"

"In a circle."

"Tell me more what they look like."

"Two are black and two are white."

"But they still dance together?"

"And they sing."

"What they sing?"

"Ring around the rosies."

"What?"

"The rhyme. You know. Ring around the rosies. Pocket full of posies. Ashes, ashes, we all fall down."

"Don't recollect as I know that one."

I flushed. "Of course not."

"Keep talkin'."

"They're beautiful. But they're frightening too. They dance in circles and spirals. The white girls have blonde hair. It's very long and reminds me of the color of wheat. The black girls have long hair too, only it's wild and glorious and spins away from them like skeins of wool. They wink at me sometimes."

Lorita pulled her hand away and the place on my cheek where she had touched burned. I reached to touch it, but she signaled to me to keep my arms down. She turned her back to me and the deep rising and falling of her shoulders seemed to shake the cabin. When she faced me again, I had to look away.

"You ever go with them?"

"What?"

"When they call, you ever go with them?"

"Sometimes. They call and I—I've gone before. When they were in the swamp on the rocks."

"How many times you go?"

"I can't remember. Twice, maybe?"

"Two? You sure? Two?"

I wrapped my arms around myself. "Yes."

"Don't go again."

"I can't help it sometimes. It feels like I don't have any control."

"You take control. You listen to Lorita. You go again when they call you, it be the last thing you do."

I backed away from her. Her huge presence. The cow's tongue over the door. The gris-gris dangling between her breasts. The smell of her sweat heavy on her dark skin. Outside the cabin door, I shivered and scoured the rows of pine trees for glimpses of their sunny hair, of their dark skin, for the sound of their small voices. Nothing. Just the dryness of my own tongue and the echo of the nursery rhyme in my thoughts.

Ashes, ashes
We all fall down.

Roberta du Bois

The day my father gave me away to Jonathan du Bois was the same day Mister Chapman over at Harlan's Plantation had three of his slaves hung for gathering together and dancing. Our wedding was on a Saturday at 3:00 in the afternoon. Everyone thought I was the luckiest girl in the world. Jonathan had the biggest house around, owned the most slaves, and was on a straight and narrow path to Congress. Daddy thought the world of him. "A true gentleman," he'd tell me time and again. "Roberta, darling, you are going to have a wonderful life."

Perhaps by my daddy's standards I did have a wonderful life, what few months were left of it after the marriage. I had enough to eat. I had beautiful clothes to wear. I worked hard though. Managing the household was no tiny task. There was always something—from dealing with the livestock to making candles to overseeing the kitchen to keeping the books. I knew down to the grain how much rice we produced. How much sack cloth we bought for the slaves' clothes, how much tallow for the candles. I knew more about the workings of that plantation than my husband. He was much more interested in acquiring more property and tossing his hat in the ring for Congress.

Over two hundred people attended our wedding. Everyone was dressed to the hilt. Unfortunately, the weather didn't cooperate, and it was a scorching ninety-two degrees that afternoon. It didn't take long for the flowers on the ladies' hats to wilt and the gentlemen to unbutton their topcoats and mop their foreheads with the linen handkerchiefs Claudia and I had spent the previous day pressing into perfect squares. Daddy looked so happy I thought he was going to burst. He kept hugging me, pressing his rough cheek against mine, exhaling his whiskey breath under my nose. "Your mother and I are so proud of you." He stumbled and held onto my shoulder. Mother stared out the window.

Oh, Daddy. I wonder what you're saying now. I wonder whether you understood at all, or if you are just furious. Like Jonathan.

I sat on my whitewashed front porch in my favorite wicker rocking chair and watched the sun set over the creek that meandered through the yard. Night approached, and with darkness, the usually muted sounds from the slave shacks grew louder. Inside, I heard Sarah and Paulette preparing supper. The clanking of the silver and the smells of pork and warm bread from the kitchen made my stomach rumble. I fanned myself with the paper in my left hand, my eye once again catching the scrawled words I already knew by heart.

Wanted Alive! $100 Reward for the return of Negro Slave, MARCUS, Property of Hon. James MacGuire. He is very dark-skinned, with a scar in the shape of an "S" around his thigh. He is about 32 years of age. 6 feet, 3 inches tall. He has a deep voice and may be wearing a blue cotton shirt stolen from my plantation. The above reward will be given with all reasonable charges for apprehending him to any prison or jail within the U. States. All persons are hereby warned against harboring or entertaining him, or of being instrumental to his escape, under the most rigorous penalties of the law. Hon. James MacGuire. 24 May, 1849. Charleston, S.C.

A sketched drawing of the man filled the center of the page. I knew him. He lay, this moment, in the shack of Morrey and Brenda, the farthest shack from the main house. I brought him food each evening after my husband retired to the study to smoke his tobacco and read.

"Missus?" Claudia stood behind me holding out a glass of lemonade. "Thought you's thirsty."

I took the glass. Claudia bowed her head and stepped backwards two steps. I drank deep. "Have you seen Master today?"

Claudia shook her head. "I hear he out lookin' for the runaway."

I pressed my lips together. "Yes. I hear that too."

In the twilight, Claudia's skin was the color of walnuts, her eyes bright. I almost reached for her, but scratched my neck instead. Claudia was my half sister. We had played together by the creek fifteen years ago. We had picked wildflowers together and followed bees to their hives. We had slept together on the grass, childs' hands clasped, sisters under the sun.

One morning I had gone to look for Claudia to pick blueberries together when Mother stopped me at the door.

"Time for playing with that child is past. She's got work she's got to do now."

I have never forgotten the ice in my mother's eyes that morning. I had never seen such coldness. Mother grabbed me by the arm and marched me into the parlor where she sat me on the piano stool. My feet couldn't reach the ground.

"That child has got no business with you," she said. "Claudia belongs with her mother and she belongs working. She's a slave girl. It's time you were paying attention to this."

I held the basket I had selected for the blueberries tight between my palms. "Claudia is my sister."

The room seemed to shrink, the walls pressing against me, making me feel even smaller than I was. Mother slapped me and the surprise of the blow made me drop the basket. "You are never to say those words again, is that clear?"

I nodded, but refused to speak.

"Get upstairs."

I fled from the parlor and up the stairs into the room I shared with my older sister Abigail. Annie, Claudia's mother, was in the bedroom making the beds. I crashed into her, then pushed her away and flung myself on the bed, wrinkling the brightly colored quilt.

"Miss, what the matter?" asked Annie.

I sobbed, pressing my wet face into the clean pillowcases Annie had just placed on the bed.

"Miss Roberta, come now and tell me."

I turned over and stared at Annie's black face. Her lips were cracked and wide, her eyes dull. Annie wore a loose fitting dress and a red and yellow bandana around her head. "Annie, my mother told me—" Tears welled up again and I choked.

Annie wiped my nose with the hem of her dress. "You can tell Annie."

"Mother told me Claudia wasn't my sister."

Annie stiffened and moved a few inches away from me. "She tole you that, did she?"

I nodded, sniffed. "I know she is. I know. My daddy tells me."

Annie's lips seemed to darken, and I became frightened. "Child, it's better this way."

"No! Claudia's my best friend! Mother wants to make her a slave!"

Annie sighed. "Miss Roberta, Claudia be my child. Claudia be a slave girl. Just like me. Just like my mama. Just like us all."

"She doesn't have to be. I can tell my daddy and he'll make it all right."

"Miss, I don't think your daddy got one concern for it one way or other."

"Yes he does! He'll do it for me!"

Annie stroked my hair and wiped another tear. "Your daddy made up his mind a long time ago that it weren't none of his concern." Annie stood up. "I been talkin' too long. Gonna get to work. You get yourself outside and get some air."

I lay on the bed where I slept each and every night and knew something inside me had fallen apart, like when Annie dropped the vase that was a gift from Mother's mother, and they were finding tiny pieces of glass on the floor for months.

"I don't suppose my husband is going to find anyone tonight," I said.

"No, ma'am," said Claudia.

The dinner bell rang, shrill and quick. "I best be goin' on," said Claudia.

"Of course." I handed the half empty glass to her. "Drink up."

She smiled and vanished into the big house. I watched the fireflies light up in the wisteria that surrounded the porch. If I allowed myself to think it, they reminded me of stars with their cool, untouchable light.

When I had found the runaway, his skin was foaming from the beating he had lived through before his escape. The soles of his feet were split to the bone and his jaw hung loose in his skull. I had touched his cheek and the man didn't have the strength to react at all. I cupped his head in my hands and looked into his bloodshot eyes, wild with pain, and whispered, "Follow me. I will protect you." Perhaps because the man had no other opportunities, perhaps because the pain pulsing through his body was simply too much to bear, or perhaps because my eyes were full of pain a different kind, he followed me.

He told me he had taken a jar of peach preserves because his wife was nearly starving. His master had imprisoned him and whipped him and tied him to a spit below a fire where hot pork fat dripped onto his open back. I instructed Morrey and Brenda to come for me if he worsened. I gave them brine and clean rags to bandage his wounds and crept quickly back into the night.

Now, at suppertime, I slid my rocking chair away from the porch's edge and entered the house. The kerosene lamps blazed. My heels tapped on the hardwood floors and I knew the kitchen slaves heard me coming. When I entered the dining room, the five slaves lined the far wall. "Master du Bois will not be joining me this evening," I said.

As if released from the pull of marionette strings, the five women relaxed and even smiled a bit as they cut up the pork and slid a slice onto my plate. I took the spoon from the mashed potatoes and scooped up a generous helping. "Perfect, as usual, Sarah."

One of the slave women blushed. "Thank you ma'am."

"You all go on into the kitchen and eat. I'll be just fine in here all by myself. I'll let you know if I hear my husband."

The women backed out of the dining room and I heard their whispers in the kitchen as they dished out the leftover meat and potatoes to take home to their own children. I hated that these women were even here at all. As long as they were in my care, I could at least keep them alive. Unfortunately, I couldn't be sure Jonathan would do the same.

The first time Jonathan saw me, after Daddy had left us alone, he made me turn around and show him my back, which so pleased him that he dared to pat my bottom. My eyes stung, but I would not flinch. Daddy had promised me to him. It had been done. I squeezed my fists together so tightly, my nails left ridges in my flesh.

"Nice," said Jonathan. He spun me back around and his eyes traveled from my forehead to my feet, lingering at my breasts. "You will do fine. I will notify your father that I have accepted his dowry," he paused, "and his daughter, and I shall send for you directly."

Jonathan left the room. The heat from his skin still pricked my flesh. I couldn't catch my breath, and held onto the back of the parlor chair so as not to collapse entirely. How could Daddy have given me to this man? Ever since the night of his wedding anniversary when I had hesitated to punish Claudia, he had abandoned me. I felt it in the power of his gaze and the absence of his touch. But this? Surely he had one ounce of compassion. Jonathan du Bois was known throughout the region for his extreme cruelty to his slaves. I knew I could expect nothing better for myself.

Daddy entered the room, smiling. "Mr. du Bois has agreed to marry you," he said. "I should think you are most pleased. He's a wealthy man with many land holdings."

My eyes narrowed. "He is a beast and he shall not touch me."

Daddy approached me and I noticed his green eyes had the same wild touch of the devil I saw in Jonathan's blue eyes. "He shall do as he pleases with you because you will be his wife. I have given a generous dowry and it will do you good to be away from this house."

I closed my eyes and whispered, "Please, may I take Claudia and Annie?"

Daddy scratched his chin. I hoped he'd realize he could be rid of all of us in one decision. "Very well. They will go with you. Now go prepare yourself to move into your husband's home. The wedding will take place in two weeks." He left the room, trailing the scent of cigar smoke and sweat.

"Very well," I said to no one in particular, gathered my skirts and walked upstairs.

Jonathan dressed in his finest suit and top hat. We held the wedding at Idyllic Grove as a sort of welcoming gesture to me. The house was splendid. Kerosene lamps and candles lined the walls. Flowers of every variety, including some imported tulips from Holland, were placed on all the tables and in huge heaping piles along the porch and staircase. I had watched as the arrangements were being made. I wanted to help, but had felt apprehensive. It wasn't my home yet. These people milling around preparing for my wedding did not know me at all. These people were perhaps wondering what kind of mistress I would be. How could they stand it? I knew my thoughts were a luxury of my skin color. Claudia had helped me dress, tightening the whalebone corset with two quick tugs.

"I can't breathe," I said.

"Sorry, Miss Roberta," she said, but she didn't loosen the strings. "This your big day. You want to look your best, don't you?"

"I can't breathe!" I turned to face Claudia. I steadied myself against the wall. The straps cut into my flesh. I imagined each one of my organs collapsing.

"Don't you be so dramatic. You just got to let yourself rearrange a little. You gots to wear it, Miss. Ain't no way you're squeezing into that wedding dress without it."

Claudia's clothing was ill-fitted. Her body hung against the blue fabric, new breasts loose and fleshy. Her belly, although slim, still swelled into a round half moon. I gasped for air, wishing for a moment for the loose dirty clothes on Claudia's back.

When I began to breathe again, if not normally at least regularly, the room took on a lighter quality, as if my lack of oxygen somehow affected the density of everything around me. When Claudia spoke, her voice sounded soft and hollow. "Miss Roberta, why you bring me here with you? Why you not leave me with your mama?"

My back was to Claudia so she could hook the buttons on my dress. "I just wanted you with me. That's all."

"You afraid to come here, ain't you? You afraid of him."

I thought of the moment we had met in Daddy's parlor. His pink skin, dusted with angry red freckles. His blue eyes rimmed with lashes so pale they appeared translucent. The way his gaze traveled up my body, lingering on my breasts and lips. I nodded.

"You love him?"

"No," I straightened my spine as Claudia fastened the last button around my neck collar.

"Your daddy want this."

"My daddy wants me out of his house. He wants me to be some other man's problem."

Claudia whispered. "I scared too."

"Why? You'll be with me."

Claudia's lips curled up into a sad smile. "Miss Roberta, you can't protect me and mama. You don't know what your husband's gon' do. At least at home, we know your mama and daddy. We know what they about. What if he separate us? What if he sell mama? There ain't nothing you can do about it, neither. Don't pretend likes you can."

I wanted to open my arms and embrace Claudia, but I was hampered by the tightness of the wedding dress and by my own inability to know how to touch my sister. If Claudia felt the same urge, she didn't act on it. "I don't know what I can do, Claudia. I wish I were a man."

"No, you don't wish that. You don't want the burden of this evil place on your shoulders for eternity. You know you can wash your hands of it. This ain't your doing. You a woman."

"Is that what you think? I don't have any responsibility for all this?"

Claudia lifted the heavy veil and arranged it over my head. "I don't know. I guess I do think you could do something."

"Don't you see? That's why I wanted to make sure you and Annie were with me! I wanted to make sure I could at least see you and try to take care of you. I know I can't do everything I should be able to. I just had hoped that maybe I could watch out for you. I don't know." Every word I could think of was false. Privileged. "Claudia, you're family."

Claudia roughly fastened the veil onto my head with bobby pins. She tugged at it, pulling my hair. "Family," she hissed and pulled the veil over my face.

When I stood at the top of the stairs, the house quieted. Only the too-loud voice of Daddy laughing with Jonathan reverberated, and even they hushed when they saw me. Mother whispered one thing before she disappeared into the back of the house. "It's going to matter to you when he's gone."

Did she mean Daddy or Jonathan?

My dress shimmered with tiny mother-of-pearl ornaments. My waist curved fashionably into a hand's span, thanks to the whale-bone corset, and the train trailed me to the top of the stairs, where Claudia held the heavy fabric. I turned my head to look at the great room. Everything sparkled. The guests holding their crystal goblets of white wine, the kerosene lamps flickering against the white walls, the gleam from the polished silver I had watched the slaves working on into the night. The combined smell of all the flowers, the liquor, and the pig roasting in the yard, made me heady and I gripped onto the banister. Daddy separated himself from Jonathan and waited for me at the foot of the stairs.

"You look exquisite, darling," he smiled, the tips of his handle-bar moustache reaching almost to his ears. He held out his hand, and on his cue, the organist began to play. I tried to control my breathing so I would at least make it down the stairs without falling. Step down, pause. Step down, pause. Through the white gauze of the veil, the room took on an unearthly hue. Even the slaves looked dusted with a pale web. Mother had appeared, as if by magic, on the left side of the room, pale face stoic. She watched me with the same disinterest she would watch a hen pecking in the yard. I found no comfort in that face or the still-smiling face of Daddy waiting at the foot of the stairs. Jonathan had seen fit to set down his wine glass, and he waited, hands behind his back, face turned toward his bride-to-be, red moustache concealing a confident smile. He didn't even look handsome dressed up.

Looking down at Daddy, I was filled with cool rage that centered in my gut before spilling into my veins. He sentenced me to this for money. I briefly entertained the idea of running from the house and somehow getting into the heart of the city, where I had heard about places where women were paid for their services. At least then I would be able to keep the money. I didn't even know what those things were that men paid for. Whatever they were, I was going to have to do them with Jonathan. Jonathan rocked on his heels. He knew what they were and was eager for tonight.

Last night, when I lay for the last time in my childhood bed, I had allowed my fingers to glide over my skin to the area underneath my breasts, the dip under my arm, the hollow at the base of my throat. I had never touched my own body before, except to bathe, and I kept listening for someone's footsteps on the stairs who would catch me doing the unthinkable. The hairs on my body rose to meet my fingers. I traced a line down the center of my belly, diving into my belly button, pulling away at the sharpness of the sensation. I rested my hands beside my body, breathing slowly, trying not to fall asleep. As soon as sleep came, morning came, and with morning, my whole world would change. Would he touch my skin gently? Honor it because it was a part of me? Or would I become his property? I rolled onto my side and stared at the blank window. The shutters were closed and I only saw the brief reflection of myself in the mirror from the flickering candlelight.

This day, Jonathan stood prepared to take his bride. I was dressed in all the finery appropriate to the occasion, but felt as if I were wearing chains. I laid my hand on Daddy's arm and smiled at him, swallowing my feelings once again. I thought of the days spent playing with Claudia, the nights spent laughing under the quilts when Annie told ghost stories from that far-off country Africa.

Daddy tightened his grip. Everyone was watching. I stretched my lips back into a smile and tried to bring that smile up to my eyes. The heavy dress tugged at my waist, even though Claudia held the train. Sweat dripped from the base of my skull, under the high collar, down my spine. I thought I saw flies buzzing around the buffet spread. Jonathan did not look at me, but instead, smiled at Daddy.

I barely heard the music. It was as if I were walking under water. The flower girl, Jonathan's niece, had scattered rose petals down the aisle. She turned back to get my approval, her blue eyes gleaming with pride at her job well done. That poor girl wishes she were me, and I almost laughed.

We reached the end of the aisle. The music stopped. Daddy gave my hand to Jonathan and moved off to the side with Mother. Through the veil's curtain, I saw Jonathan's face, lips thin and straight, nose crooked, bent to the right as if it had been broken in a fight. His fingers tightened around mine and I thought of the corset, and felt again its hardness against my bones.

This was supposed to be the happiest day of my life. I whispered that over and over to myself. This was it. The culmination of my entire childhood to be exchanged with two words in an overly decorated parlor. This man's fingers felt cold even through my glove. This was it. This was the remainder of my life.

"Do you, Jonathan du Bois, take this woman, Roberta Saunders, to be your lawfully wedded wife?" The pastor scratched his beard.

"I do."

"And do you, Roberta Saunders, take this man, Jonathan du Bois, to be your lawfully wedded husband, to love, honor and obey him until death do you part?"

I blinked. I didn't remember the preceding parts of the ceremony. Now it was up to this. I nodded before I spoke. "I do." I was sure the back of my dress was a pattern of sweat.

"In the name of the Lord God Almighty, and his Son Jesus Christ Our Lord, I now pronounce you husband and wife. You may kiss the bride."

I lowered my head as Jonathan lifted the veil. He placed his index finger under my chin and tilted my head up to meet his. I thought I felt a snake in my mouth before I realized it was his tongue. I closed my teeth on it.

Eating alone in the dining room was rather pleasant. The usual sharp words I heard from Jonathan were blessedly absent this evening. It would be easier for me to get food to the runaway if Jonathan were otherwise occupied. I had aided three other Negroes in this same manner. I could not help as much as I would have liked because it would be too dangerous and I could not jeopardize what little consolation I could offer. I took a bite of pork. By Providence my skin was white. I knew, even at eighteen, my actions in this skin must be my own responsibility. I felt I could surely endure the wifely duties that were my lot in life if they afforded me information about the slave traders and the auctions by the wharf. Jonathan was often prone to unusual bits of conversation when he was tugging at my flesh.

"Claudia!" I called.

Claudia appeared almost instantly in the hall. "Yes, ma'am?"

"Get together a plate of this pork and some hominy and wrap it up tight for me."

"Yes, ma'am." Claudia vanished.

I traced the pattern on the china plate with my fork. It looked as if I could take another journey to Morrey and Brenda's cabin that evening. Maybe Jonathan was not even searching for this man. Perhaps someone else had escaped. Claudia returned with the plate of food, wrapped in a white and red towel. "Thank you," I said.

Claudia nodded and set the plate down on the table.

"If my husband returns, tell him I have gone walking and will return shortly."

"Yes, ma'am." Claudia began to clear the table, leaving one place setting for Jonathan's return.

I stepped out of the house, grateful to breathe the heavy, fragrant air. Although cooler inside, the house often seemed oppressive to me. I much preferred the outdoors where I could see clearly the demons that haunted me. Inside, the demons often hid in crevices I could not see until it was too late. Two Negroes playing cards on a tree stump in the moonlight nodded at me.

"Evenin', missus," said the older one. He wore a felt hat with a hole over his right ear.

"Good evening," I replied and walked past them. I heard them shuffle their cards and deal again.

The walk to Morrey and Brenda's cabin was more treacherous in the evening because of snakes. Their cabin sat low by the Snaky Swamp and was often surrounded by cottonmouths and water moccasins. The thick net of mosquitoes often kept Jonathan from venturing this far onto his property. I slapped at a mosquito that had landed on my neck and instantly regretted the dab of rose oil I'd placed behind my ears that morning. Clumps of tobacco burned around the cabin to try to keep the mosquitoes away from the door. I approached quietly, looking around me for any sign I may have been followed.

"Brenda?" I whispered. "It's me."

The cabin door slid open and Brenda poked her head around the corner. "Missus?"

I pushed the door the rest of the way open and entered the stifling hot cabin. Morrey sat along the wall on a stool made from pine wood. The fugitive lay in their bed, shaking. "I brought some more food. Some for you all, too."

Brenda took the plate. "We thankful."

The man's chest rose and fell, each exhale a rattle of breath. Each inhale the dragging of irons. "His notice was posted today. My husband went to help round him up. I don't know how much longer he will be safe here."

"Do you know his name?" asked Brenda.

"Marcus."

Morrey grunted. "They gon' set the bloodhounds out for him."

I knelt beside the bed. "I don't see what else they can do to him."

"Miss Roberta, they be many things worse than death." Brenda tore a piece of the pork and gave it to Morrey.

"I suppose you're right." I wiped the man's forehead. The sweat was tinted red. His breathing rocked his bones. "He's in no condition to move. There might be a boat that could take him on up to Massachusetts where he might be safe. But he can't travel alone."

Morrey stood up. He was tall—too tall for the cabin. He stooped his shoulders. "Missus, you best be gettin' on back. We tend to him."

My gaze lingered on Morrey's scarred face. Two jagged cuts traced each cheek. He had a vertical wound on his neck that still oozed fluid. Each of his fingers bent peculiarly so his hands appeared more like claws.

"Got me the arthritis," he said. "Hard but I keep pickin'."

I looked away. I knew I had to get home. There was no telling when Jonathan would arrive, and he would expect his wife to be waiting for him. I stood, letting my hand linger on the sleeping man's face. "God bless." I took the plate and towel back from Brenda, lest anyone find them among their things. Brenda had already transferred the food to her own plates.

"Hurry on now, Miss Roberta," said Brenda.

"Good night." I left the cabin, stepping carefully on the damp soil. The moon was full, which was both a blessing and a curse. I could be much more easily seen in this light. I had just rounded the bend that put me on a direct track to the great house when I heard a noise from the side of the road. I clutched my plate tight to my chest and kept walking.

"Psst! Miss Roberta!" The voice hesitated. "Miss Roberta!"

I stopped and turned around. "Who's there?"

Claudia stepped out from behind a pine tree, brushing pine needles off her shoulders. She was wearing a black cloak and her head was wrapped with a black cloth.

"Claudia! What are you doing out here! You have to get back!"

I pushed her back into the trees. "What if the overseers or the constable catch you? It's well after the nine o'clock curfew."

"I know, Miss Roberta, but I has to come." Claudia's gaze was traveling quickly from me to the trees to the swamp. She hunched her shoulders, as if afraid for the next blow. "He back."

I didn't know what I should do. I had to get Claudia back home and inside. As for myself, I didn't know what I'd say. "I can just tell him I've been out walking. He knows I enjoy the evenings."

"Miss Roberta, he say he seen you carryin' food someplace. I thinks he gon' hurt you."

I closed my eyes. "No, Claudia," I sighed. "He won't hurt me. It doesn't look right."

"I don' know, ma'am. I ain't never seen him quite like this before. He scarin' all of us."

What if Jonathan had seen me? What would he do? What would happen to Brenda and Morrey? I had to believe Claudia was overreacting. Jonathan could be frightening for no good reason, and this must simply be one of those times. Still, I best not waste any more time.

"You get on back to the house, Claudia, and I thank you."

Claudia ran into the forest, as soundless as sunset.

When I approached the big house, light shone from every window. Men milled around the porch, some with rifles cocked over their shoulders, others with a bottle of whiskey or a cigar in their hands. There was a low hum to their conversation, like a beehive, and I was loath to disturb them. I needn't have worried. Jonathan saw me first. I had given the plate and towel to Claudia, who promised to dispose of them where no one would find them. I walked empty-handed toward the house.

"Well, if it isn't the prodigal wife," said Jonathan. Some of the men laughed. "Where you been?"

"Just out for a walk." I wiped my hands on my dress. "You know how I love to enjoy the night air."

"Just out for a walk. Ain't you worried about catchin' the fever?" He stood in front of me. Head to head, we were of equal height. He grabbed my shoulders. "Who accompanied you?"

"No one, Jonathan. I enjoyed my own company."

He pushed me against the porch rail. "The hell you did." He spit on my face. I dared not move to wipe it off. "I know you're taking care of some nigger. I hear things, Roberta. I know you think I'm stupid, but I know what is going on on my own land, and I damn well know what my own wife is doing! Have I made myself clear?"

"Perfectly." I leaned against the railing until I steadied myself and could stand face to face with him again. "How dare you accuse me of undermining your authority. I know my place." I pushed against him and walked into the house.

Jonathan let out a scream that reminded me more of a trapped animal than a man, and he leapt on me from behind, knocking me to the ground. He turned me on my back and slapped me across the face so hard my ears rang. "Don't you ever walk away from me when I am talking to you."

I kicked his shins, turned onto my stomach and crawled on all fours toward the kitchen. The men had gathered around the front door and were watching through the windows. I raised myself up, but Jonathan caught me from behind and I fell forward, striking my chin against a table. I tasted hot blood. He pulled my hair loose from its pins and jerked my head back.

"I'll break your neck, you do anything like this again. Do you know who I am?"

I know exactly who you are, I thought, but I did not utter a word.

Jonathan forced my legs apart, lifted my skirts up, and raised my hips in the air. The men on the porch cheered and clinked their glasses together. I heard Jonathan fumbling at his trousers and I closed my eyes. Silence. Silence. I must stay silent.

The sounds from the men on the porch faded in my mind and all that was real to me was the square foot of flooring inches from my face. Scuffs from riding boots and tiny initials "G.H." marked the wood. My insides ached and I was sure blood was trickling down my thighs but I did not speak. He finished, pushed me prone on the floor and kicked me with the toe of his boot right at the base of my spine.

"Now," he said. "Go get Claudia."

Claudia was eleven. I was fourteen. It was February, 1855, half a decade since Claudia and I played together behind the big house. Mother had decided I needed to begin learning some responsibility for the household slaves. Daddy knew Mother hated Annie and Claudia, so to ensure they were both kept as far away from her as possible, he made them my charges.

We were celebrating Mother and Daddy's twentieth wedding anniversary. Pierce Mason Butler, the governor of South Carolina, was expected to attend. The party was scheduled for three days, culminating with a hog roast on Saturday. All of us were busy. Mother was up each morning at four to begin the day's work. She expected nothing less of me or our slaves.

Over fifty people stood in our front room when it happened. Men and women wearing stiff fabrics, hats of all colors and sizes, gloves so white they shone. Hoop skirts made the room an obstacle course. The windows were gray with condensation. Outside, the sun shone thin and yellow through the crisp winter air.

Claudia was carrying a heavy silver tray loaded with Mother's best china tea setting when she tripped on the woven oval rug. The tray was wider than her young body. She fell, dropped the tray, broke the china, and sent scalding water across the chest of the governor's wife. The seconds of absolute stillness before the governor's wife regained enough composure to shout reverberated through the house.

Annie rushed to her daughter and began to start to clean up. Claudia, dazed from the fall, was speechless.

"Roberta!" Mother shouted. "Take control of your slaves!" She turned to the governor's wife, whose wrinkled face was flushed from pain or anger or both. "I do apologize. I assure you, she will be dealt with. Roberta!"

I saw little Claudia's face, now registering the gravity of her mistake. My baby sister.

"Roberta!" It was Daddy now. The men were watching him, pipes in hand, to see if his reputation was deserved. "Take care of it."

"Yes, sir." I knelt by Claudia and suppressed the urge to stroke her hair. "Claudia!" I tried to shout, but it came out weak.

"Oh for heaven's sake," Mother marched over to me, yanked Claudia up by her arm and held her hand over the half-empty tea pitcher. The water steamed. Claudia whined like a puppy. "You'll not be so clumsy again." She thrust Claudia's hand into mine. "Put it in the water."

Claudia's pulse thumped in her wrist. I had to pull her just to keep her standing. All of Mother and Daddy's guests watched me.

"Roberta," said Mother. "Put her hand in the water."

Claudia sucked in air. She tried to remain still. My baby sister. Daddy cleared his throat. I closed my eyes and forced her eleven-year old hand into the scalding water. She screamed and pulled back so hard that by reflex I pulled harder and held her hand under the water too long. When I finally released her, her hand was shaking, the skin already blistering. I thought of the way the fresh-caught crabs screamed when they were thrown in the iron kettle of boiling water. Claudia backed away, pressing against Annie's legs. Annie held her hand over her daughter's mouth.

"She'll be more careful now," said Mother.

People backed away from me. Annie knelt to clean up the shattered glass. My own hands shook; the heat from the boiling water caused them to sweat. Claudia. Mother was proud. Justice had been served. Order preserved.

I walked up the rounded staircase to my room and lay down on the bed Claudia had just made that morning. If I had had courage, I would have cut my own wrists. But I didn't, and I lay there on the cool quilt, the sun bright in my eyes, my own skin smooth and untouched as fresh snow.

The Swamp Sirens

"You see her just do that?" Number One whispered to Number Two.

"Now's the time!" said Number Three.

Ring around the rosies
Pocket full of posies
Ashes, ashes
We all fall down!

"She held her hand in the water," said Number Two.

"She crossed over to the dark place."

"Tonight is the night."

"We can get her tonight."

"Dance with us!"

"Miss Roberta! Come dance with us!"

The four girls in faded yellow pinafores joined hands, a human chain, and stretched from the top of the pine tree outside Roberta's window to her windowsill. Number Three hung onto the shutter and waved at the figure lying on the bed.

"Hey!" said Number Three. "Roberta!"

The fourteen-year-old on the bed did not move. The girls were not even sure she was breathing.

"She wouldn't have just gone without us," said Number Four.

"No, no," said Number One. "She would have told us. At the very least."

The girl on the bed held her hands out in front of her, turning them, one by one, at the wrist. She touched the palm of her left hand with her right fingertips, then separated, then connected, as if strands of glue stretched through her pores.

"There's a party downstairs," said Number Two.

"She better get back down there," said Number One.

"Roberta!"

"Do you want to come play with us?"

The girl on the bed reached her arms above her head, lowered them, and inhaled so deeply the girls could see her chest rise.

Seconds passed.

"She needs to let it out," said Number Three.

"Maybe she's trying this way," said Number One.

"No. Not like this. A person can't hold her own breath. Some-one else has to do that for her," said Number Four.

Number Three pressed her face against the glass. The girl on the bed sat up, looked straight at Number Three, and lay back down.

"She knows we're here," said Number Three.

Number Three leaped from the windowsill to the lowest branch of the pine tree. The four girls hung like icicles in the branches.

"I think my shoe is caught," said Number One.

Ring around the rosies
Pocket full of posies

"Come on! Let's dance for her!" said Number Two.

"One! Two! Three!" They shouted and pushed away from the tree and spun, heels kicking up behind them.

Ashes, ashes
We all fall down!

The girl on the bed stood, crossed to the window, blew a kiss at the dancing girls, and drew the shade.

Roberta du Bois

Every so often, there's more than Gabriel and me here in the walls. Every so often, some of the others come. When they do, I know absolutely that God doesn't let anybody get away with anything. I know God calls us all to account, one way or another. Nobody leaves clean.

I have never been able to see the others who come to Gabriel, but the ones who come to me are the same two who came to me in life: Annie, our slave and my father's lover, and Claudia, my slave sister and my husband's lover. They don't ever seem mad too much. Claudia will sit and talk with me for quite a spell. It's like she wants me to know everything that happened to her. Maybe she thinks it'll cure me, or kill me. The line is thin.

Annie hardly ever speaks, but she doesn't need to. When I see her, gray hair tied behind her neck in a dirty towel, I remember how fiercely she loved Claudia. I remember how she was somehow able to be cordial to me, and now, in both our deaths, we stand at the same crossroad. She's on one side of the gate, waiting for something. I'm on the other side of the gate, waiting as well. Perhaps we're waiting for the same thing. Sometimes Claudia shares my tobacco. Other times she talks. I don't talk too much. I'm afraid if I do, she'll go away, and I'll have to admit that, although I enjoy Lillian and Hannah, I much prefer the company of the dead.

Dear Mommy,

Did you know we aren't supposed to take Roberta away from the house? If you did, it was mean of you not to tell me. I thought I would have the best show and tell of anyone in the class. Instead, they laughed at me and no one, not one, could see her, even though she put an extra feather in her hat so she'd be pretty. I pointed right at her, but all they saw was air.

Are we crazy, Mommy? Because that's what they say.

Love,
Hannah
Age 8

Roberta du Bois

The walls and I heard Claudia and Annie's story about Faith's birth over and over and over. It was as if their sole purpose in hanging around was to keep telling me what happened. When they spoke, I couldn't interrupt. I could only listen and remember my own mistakes. Each time I heard the story, my snakebites puckered and wept.

Faith had arrived too soon. I thought that was the only concern. I didn't know then that Jonathan was the father. I didn't know that he had sought her out before we were even married. I didn't know that when I walked down that staircase to marry Jonathan, that Claudia, still a child, was already pregnant with his child. So much I never saw, never let myself see.

Claudia heard cloth ripping in the other room. Someone had gone to the well for water. When she opened her eyes again, she was surrounded by women. Annie knelt at the foot of the cot, massaging Claudia's feet. Paulette had a rag dripping with cool water pressed to her forehead.

"Too early, Mama," said Claudia.

"Nonsense. It's the perfect time," said Annie. Claudia couldn't see her mother's face because a flash of pain penetrated her body. She saw red, closed her eyes and moaned.

Paulette had called for me, for what little I could do.

Annie reached her hands up under Claudia's hips and pulled her gently toward the edge of the cot. She inserted her fingers into Claudia and pulled them out so quickly Claudia gasped. Annie stood up and walked toward the window. She motioned for Sarah. Sarah followed, glancing back at Claudia.

"What is it, Annie?"

"I felt its feet. That child is backwards. This is nothin' but a trouble sign."

Claudia' saw the room spin, although she knew she was lying flat on the cot. The whole room tilted at wide angles, and she wondered why the dishes weren't falling out of the cabinets in the next room. "I'm gon' die," she whispered. "Mama! Mama, I'm gon' die!"

Annie stopped rinsing her hands in the pail of hot water and turned to her daughter. "Get some whiskey," she said to Sarah, before kneeling on the wooden floor beside Claudia's cot. "You, my child, are not gon' die. Good Lord never gives us more than we can bear. What you need to do is concentrate and you help me now. This gon' hurt and there ain't a thing I can do about it. If I don't take this child out of you, it is gon' kill you and I don't want you even thinkin' about leavin' me here all alone, you hear me?"

Claudia's back ached and she thought maybe her wounds had opened back up again and she was flowing blood out the back and front of her. That image struck her as funny, and she tried to laugh, but only managed a weak chuckle. Annie stood and went back to get the knife. Sarah returned with a bottle of whiskey. Annie nodded toward Claudia.

"Here, honey," said Sarah. "Drink up."

Claudia raised her head as best she could. She felt like a thousand knives were slicing through her insides. How did they think they could hurt her with one more? She took a swallow. It was strong and burned her throat. She turned her head away. "No more."

"You gots to drink all this up." Sarah lifted Claudia's head and began to pour the whiskey into her mouth. Claudia choked and spat it back, but Sarah was persistent. Soon Claudia's head was heavy on her neck and it was hard to breathe. Annie brought a damp cloth and pressed it on Claudia's forehead. "My child, my child."

"Mama?" Claudia's lips felt thick. "Don't make it hurt too bad."

"Baby, I promise you. You done been through worse."

Claudia never knew exactly when she passed out. She always remembered a wave of pain from the base of her spine and then her next memory was of Annie, Sarah and me standing around her, each with her own expression of sadness, or was it rage? She could never be quite sure. The faces blurred in front of her.

"No, no, honey. Stay here." It was Annie. Annie always knew what to say, she thought, and closed her eyes. Annie sat on the edge of the cot and kissed her daughter's cheek. Through half-open eyelids, Claudia saw the layers of blood on her clothes. She listened, as if from a far-away fog, but heard no cries.

She suddenly noticed how dry her throat was and how silent the room was. "Where's my baby?"

I knelt beside the cot and put one hand on Annie's knee, the other on Claudia's thigh. "Claudia, your baby—well, Paulette took your baby out of the room for awhile so you could get some rest."

"Your baby was born with a caul around her eyes. She gon' to be special," said Annie.

Claudia tried to move, but fell back against the hard cot. Her belly was still large. Annie stroked Claudia's hair.

"She a girl?"

"She a girl." Annie's gaze traveled to mine.

"I name her Faith," said Claudia.

Annie exhaled. "Darlin', there's somethin' you need to know."

"What's wrong? What's wrong with my baby? Bring her to me!"

"You need your rest, right now," I said. "There's nothing wrong with your baby. She's absolutely beautiful." I nodded to Annie.

"Child, your baby is white as a ghost. Flaming red hair. Eyes as blue as sky." Annie gripped Claudia's hand.

The realization of what that meant traveled over Claudia slowly, like a cold reptile. Child follows the state of the mother. Child a slave. Jonathan won't have a white child in bondage on his property. He'd send her off. Else he'd kill her. Claudia's own skin was so dark it looked red in moonlight. Her eyes so brown they were black. Jonathan must have done something to her to make her have a white baby.

I stood. "Claudia, I don't know how I am going to fix this. I have to go think about it. Until then, I will tell my husband that you are still in labor and that he is not to disturb you for any reason."

"He not gon' pay no attention to you, Miss Roberta," said Claudia.

I clasped my hands at my chest and said, "This time he will."

After I left, Sarah cleaned up the floor with rags and soap water. All that blood and fluid poured out of Claudia like she was a river. Couldn't have the floor stained like that. Sweat dripped off Sarah's forehead into the blood. Annie released Claudia's hand and dipped her own in the bucket of soap water Sarah was using. Never in all her days had she seen anything like this. What had happened that her black baby had a pasty white baby? A woman as dark as her Claudia should have a yellow baby. A tan baby. Not a white baby. This must be an omen. Spirits trying to say something. "What?" Annie whispered.

"What you say, Mama?" asked Claudia.

"Nothin', baby. I just thinkin'." Annie tried to smile, but only managed a slight frown. "You just get you some rest. I'll be back in a bit."

"Where you gon'?"

"I'm gon' see Lorita. I'll be back soon."

Claudia lay on her swollen back and looked at her swollen belly. Lorita? Sweet Jesus, what had she done?

Claudia lay on the straw bedding. A white baby girl nursed at her breast. Ghost hour outside. She heard them walking in the trees. Singing. Fly away home. Cross the river now. Fly away home. What was the song her mother sang to her? She couldn't remember.

The baby sucked hard. Claudia lowered her head to look at this bright white glowing baby, so shiny next to her own dark skin. This baby, child of her master, born to slavery. She ached. In the morning, they would bury the baby. In the morning, she and Miss Roberta would lower a rock-filled coffin into the earth. In the morning, she would hand the white baby over to Lorita.

The baby bled the milk from her. Mama? Out in the trees. Mama? Comin' for to carry me home.

Claudia pushed the baby away. It cried. She looked at it again, red-white face puckered like a corncob doll. The shrieks rocked her. One more day. Master come again. She could pull her skirt over the baby's face and end it. They were pretending anyway. Why not make it real? Why not end this child's suffering and her own before too much time passes? What kind of life are you going to have anyway, baby girl? The baby's blue eyes mocked her. She hated this child. Yet, at the same instant, she thought her compassion would overflow and pour out of her like the afterbirth. Only a few hours until morning. Miss Roberta will come soon.

"I'm so sorry," was all I could say when I got there.

Claudia stared at the earth over her swollen belly. None of it mattered. "Yes, ma'am."

I took her hand and knelt before her. I traced the surface of the burn scars with her finger. Claudia had no feeling in that hand. Not since she was eleven. Not since I took the feeling from her. "No, Claudia. Truthfully. I am so sorry." I wanted nothing more than to touch my sister's cheek, to fly backwards in time to the moments we spent gathering blackberries, laughing at a monarch butterfly's dance through the vines.

Claudia pulled her hand away. "What's done is done. Nothing can be changed."

I stood, brushed the dust from my skirts, the water from my eyes. "You stay strong."

Claudia cringed at another shriek from the baby. Claudia's so strong not even God above could break her. I had been the only one even come close. And that was so long ago, Claudia only felt it on occasion, and then in the middle of her stomach, right below her rib cage.

Claudia tossed and turned on the straw. She felt strange, lying down in daylight, and even stranger still preparing to bury a pile of stones as her little girl. The dreams came, fast and furious, every time she closed her eyes. Bright colors, red hair, darkness and blood. She didn't know what to make of it. Thought surely it was angering the spirits to be staging a death. Yet what choice did she have? There was something about this child that clung to the edges of her heart. She wondered, in that half-sleep place, what Lorita was doing with Faith now. Was the girl sleeping? Crying? Maybe Baby Faith was also under a canopy of dreams she could not begin to understand.

Claudia lay flat, listening to the sounds from the kitchen below. She heard laughter, whispers, between the rhythmic banging of the pots and chopping of the vegetables. She knew that kitchen with all her bones. Every piece of silver she had polished with her own fingers until they reflected back her tired face. Every piece of linen she had washed, sprinkled, and ironed with her own hands. She thought of the smoothness of Baby Faith's skin, so white as to be almost translucent. The red blotches around her face and neck, the trauma from the birth. The fineness of her hair, like silk thread. Claudia did not know how that child could have lived in her belly. Then she had a thought: Maybe Baby Faith could go far away to the north, and because she was so very white, she could go live the life of a little white girl. Everyone knows the north is paradise on earth. Yes. She'd talk to Lorita about arranging passage. Then she drifted into sleep again, the noises from the kitchen a backdrop to her dreams.

At dusk, I climbed the stairs and knelt beside my sister. "Hey, sweetheart," I whispered. "It's time."

Claudia, who had finally fallen into a deep sleep, was startled awake. When she saw my face, she closed her eyes again, remembering. "I'm gon' to send my baby north," she said.

"What?" I kissed her forehead. "Don't be silly. Here you can look after her. You can still see her. If you send her north, God only knows what could happen to her."

"She can be white up north." Claudia sat up and smoothed down the edges of her dress. "Nobody have to know about me."

"I don't know what to say anymore, Claudia. Everything seems so completely out of my hands."

"Missus, be grateful them hands that everything seem out of is white."

"Best get ready for the burial," I said and hurried away from the cot where Claudia lay tangled in sheets of her own thoughts.

The gray earth falling on the rock-filled coffin reminded Claudia of the thud a body makes when it is cut down from the noose. She had seen a black woman hanged in the square when she was a little girl. Her mama had told her the woman had stolen bread. Claudia remembered the absence of any expression on the woman's face as they pulled the hood over her head. They pulled the lever; she fell, arms and legs jerking up before falling against her body. The crowd, black and white, cheered. Claudia hid her face in Annie's dress. That's when she heard the sound. The body dropped the few feet to the ground, landing, a solid thud, onto the packed earth. Claudia peeked one eye out from behind the folds of the apron and saw the woman, now lying face down in the dirt, no one paying any attention to her body, no one running to help her. She was dead. Claudia knew that, in her child's mind, but she also knew something deeper then. She knew without having the words for it, that the body of a black woman was worth nothing. The laughter and joking from the spectators proved her point. Underneath a dogwood tree, a small black boy cried, kept from running to the body by another woman's hands.

With each shovel full of dirt Morrey tossed onto the box, Claudia remembered the condemned woman. What had she done? Did she only steal a loaf of bread, or did she do something worse? Did she try to stop the unwanted advances of a white man? Did she try to protect her child? It seemed like the little boy screamed for hours. Claudia didn't remember returning home that day. She remembered Master Saunders telling her he hoped she'd learned a lesson. She had nodded, but she didn't know what lesson he had hoped she would learn by watching a woman die.

Would it be worse if her child were in that box instead of rocks? What would those tears feel like? Hotter? Wetter? More salt? She grabbed Annie's hand and squeezed. Mama. What does "mama" mean in these times? Annie could be taken from her as easily as her daughter had been. As easily as that little boy's mother had been all those years ago.

Lorita stretched out her arms and drew the women closer together around the coffin and began to whisper.

"Those who are dead are never gone. They are under the earth. They are in the trees. They are in the skies. Those who are gone are never dead. They live in our hearts and in our bodies. We are all family in this flesh."

The women bowed their heads until they touched, forming a triangle over the tiny empty coffin. Lorita pressed her palms against the coffin lid, then blew on it, clapped her hands and the three women backed away. Morrey helped them lower the casket into the hole he had dug earlier.

The earth was raised where the grave lay. Claudia knelt beside it and placed a lily she had stolen from one of the vases in the big house. Faith was as good as dead. She couldn't see her. She couldn't risk both their lives like that. Perhaps that was the lesson Master Saunders had wanted her to learn. Never risk your heart. And so she hadn't. But every once in awhile, something crept in. Who'd have thought that something would be a white baby girl, born from rape?

Lorita watched Claudia, kneeling beside the lump of earth. "Don't worry, girl. I watch out for your baby. No need for tears."

Claudia had heard the sound of earth falling on a coffin many times before. The thudding made her spirit break like a mirror. When there's a body in the box, the falling dirt sounded heavier. A final insult to the dead to have dirt tossed on top of them and then to be left alone in the cold ground. How the spirit must rage, she thought, as it throws itself against the walls of its coffin. Claudia knelt beside the grave and pressed her palms into the mound of dirt, leaving two small handprints, fingers fanned out like sun's rays.

This was just about the only story Claudia and Annie seemed to know, and they were compelled to make me hear it. They were compelled to make me share in the telling of it. Over time in these walls, I sometimes can't tell one voice from the other.

Roberta du Bois

I stood on the porch steps and watched the dust rise from the fields. I heard singing, deep and loud, but I couldn't recognize the words. Jonathan forbade the slaves to sing, but he was away again and I allowed it, although it disturbed me almost as much as the mornings when Jonathan breaks up families and sells them off to different plantations. Those mornings, their voices hit my lower belly, the reverberations traveling up my spinal column, out onto the branches of my shoulders and down into my fingers, causing them to twitch rhythmically against my thighs. I thought of Claudia's Baby Faith, hiding in Lorita's cabin. She really should get off the plantation. But then, who could protect her?

When I'd held Faith after she was born, I recognized the thin mouth, the orange hair of my husband. The baby wriggled and stared at me with huge blue eyes rimmed with black lashes. I wrapped the child in a soft cotton blanket and handed her to Annie, who covered the child even further with her shawl before she slipped into the night.

When I held Baby Faith, my breasts ached. I knew the child could have been my own daughter. Perhaps I should have passed her off as my own daughter. People were talking about my inability to conceive already, even though we'd only been married a few months. Still, Faith was my niece. Nothing Jonathan could do could take that from me. Just like nothing could change the fact Claudia was my sister. And a slave.

The day of Faith's fake funeral was red. The sunrise had been crimson, backwards. Cardinals, lost perhaps, hovered around the swamp. I had convinced Jonathan to leave Claudia alone while she mourned the death of her child. As I had expected, Jonathan had no desire to see the body. I couldn't tell if he were relieved there was one less mouth to feed, or angry there would be one less slave to sell.

I stood up. At twilight, when most of the work for the day was finished, they would hold the brief ceremony. I had to concentrate on candle making. A daughter would indeed have been helpful. I'd heard talk that Jonathan's sister Edna was going to send over her oldest daughter Ida to help with the house, but so far nothing had come of it.

The field slaves started a new song, this one high-pitched and mournful. I thought of Marcus, the runaway I'd tried to help. He died on Brenda and Morrey's bed, just hours after I brought the food. Morrey had buried the body in the slave cemetery in the middle of the night on a new moon. When I saw Morrey the next day, his eyes were blank.

The day loomed in front of me like a tightrope. I wiped my brow with the back of my hand and flicked the sweat onto the porch. At least I'd managed to secure a few days of rest for Claudia. Right now, my sister was upstairs on the straw mattress outside my bed-room, sleeping, I hoped, peacefully sleeping.

I paced in the main room. Jonathan stood in the doorway, chewing on the end of his pipe, watching. He had just returned early from the auction.

"What are you so worked up about, woman?"

I smoothed my hair, tucked tightly into a French twist. "Just the usual happenings. Someone's pilfering from the dairy again. I can't seem to get a handle on the new kitchen girl. I think she will do, but one never knows."

"You having trouble with her? I'll get Saul to speak to her."

Saul was the overseer. He lived in a slightly better version of the slave shacks just south of the big house where he and his wife raised their half dozen children. Saul's people were dirt farmers. Jonathan liked him instantly because of his desperation. He knew Saul would do anything not to return to the tarpaper shack he had found him in. "A desperate man becomes your most loyal friend," his father had told him, and that proverb had proven true in the case of Saul. There was nothing he wouldn't do to ensure that Jonathan's plantation ran smoothly and efficiently. Jonathan loved to watch him work. He thought I was too squeamish on these matters.

"No, no. That won't be necessary." I stopped pacing. "I'm sure she just needs some time to adjust. She's only about eleven or so."

Jonathan exhaled blue smoke from his nostrils. "Where's Claudia?"

"Still recovering. You leave her alone right now, hear me? That woman needs to heal."

'You're too soft on her. You think of her like family. You can't do that. Don't know how many times I have to tell you. Black and white are like oil and water."

"She's a human being, Jonathan. Just like you and me."

Jonathan pushed past me. "Not like me."

I watched my husband walk out the front door. His spine was too straight. I saw none of the fluidity I saw in the backs of the slaves as they bent over the rice. None of the motion that often reminded me of waves lapping at the shore that I saw in the too few moments when the slaves danced. My hands hung useless at my side and I realized the futility of what I wanted to do. I watched him through the floor-to-ceiling window. He stood, motionless except for the puffing of his pipe, surveying all that was his. To him, I was just another asset in his ledger book.

It was time to prepare for the service. Earlier in the day, I had arranged for Morrey to bring the tiny coffin he'd already pre-filled with stones and leave it in the smokehouse draped with an old cloth. Annie and Lorita were together, tending to Baby Faith, whom they were going to have to leave bundled tightly in the corner of Lorita's cabin while the ceremony took place. I was counting on Jonathan's lack of interest.

"I was surprised to see you back today," I said. "Thought for sure that the auction would have kept you another week."

Jonathan didn't turn around. "Nothing worth buying. Got us plenty right now. They're not rounding up the kind they used to. They were all weak and sickly. The cheapest one was a hundred dollars and he had to have been eighty years old!"

"Shall I tell them you'll be here for supper?"

He leaned against one of the porch columns. "I'm going to ride over to Daddy's."

"We'll keep supper warm."

He was already off the porch and walking toward the stable when I allowed myself to exhale. I waited until he was out of earshot, stepped off the braided rug and called to Claudia. "He's gone now! Let's get moving!"

Claudia emerged at the top of the stairs, hair popping out of her head rag in spirals. She descended slowly.

"I think he'll be gone awhile. He went to his daddy's. Sure as sin they'll end up drunk before sunset."

I put my arm around Claudia's neck, but Claudia stiffened and I took it away. "I reckon I can walk on by myself."

"Of course." I stepped back and watched Claudia walk through the kitchen, past the two big stoves, past the stone fireplace, through the slave entrance into the backyard where Annie and Lorita waited. Claudia collapsed into her mother, her back heaving with the sorrow she couldn't share with me. I thought of our father. His smell of tobacco and whiskey. His thin, handlebar mustache that he trimmed compulsively in his study in front of a tiny ivory hand mirror. The largeness of his knuckles and the smallness of his nose. What, indeed, did men think about? Did they ever think about the suffering they caused?

I took the family Bible from the parlor and followed the women through the back of the house out to the slave cemetery. The walk was longer than I remembered, the dirt path muddy and overgrown with weeds and wildflowers. I watched the two women bent in front of me, each leaning on the other, and my hands ached to reach out to them. Instead, I pressed them tighter against the Bible and focused on the fact that my niece was safe with Lorita—safe from my husband.

Lorita waited for them in the clearing, her shoulders draped with a black flour sack. She wore no shoes and her hair was loose and wild. She stretched her long arms out and Claudia fell into them. "How is she?"

Lorita whispered something I couldn't hear, but it calmed Claudia, who stood back and straightened up. Annie looked to me. I didn't know quite what to do in Lorita's presence. I tried to hand her the Bible, but Lorita shook her head.

"Not for this, Miss Roberta."

I took a step backwards. I knew if these women had their way, I would not have been a part of this ceremony, fake one or not. I knew I was the laughingstock of the plantation. Everyone knew Jonathan slipped from cabin to cabin in the predawn hours, preferring my own half-sister to anyone else. I could only hold my head up because I was the mistress and there was simply no other option available.

It sickened me to feel some ping of envy. But sometimes when I saw them stealing moments of passion in the woods or jumping the broom in back of their shacks, I knew I would never in my life know a moment of such surrender. There was no one at all in my life I would risk anything for, except perhaps Claudia, and it was much too late for that. Sometimes, when I sneaked out and went walking late at night and passed a slave couple kissing, I thought I'd give every bit of privilege I had to know one moment of passion.

Ungrateful woman, I was. I was free, as free as any woman in my time and place could be. And freedom was far more important than passion, was it not?

Every time I heard the crack of Saul's whip on the back of one of the slaves, I got my answer.

Claudia and Annie held hands around the hole Morrey had dug earlier in the soft earth. Lorita walked over to me.

"Mistress, I see you, but I tell you don't you be looking for forgiveness here with us. You in the wrong place for that. Me, Annie and Claudia—this is ours."

I clutched the Bible tighter. "I just want—I don't know. I want for you to be all right. I want for Claudia to—"

Lorita touched my shoulder. "I know your heart is good, Mistress. But even you can't forget you the Mistress. How you think they goin' to forget? How do you think it feels for Claudia to know that you and her have the same daddy and yes, you even share the same husband, but still she has to stay here? Has to work in the house for you. Has to give up her babies. Has to have her mama wipe the blood from her back that your husband ordered drawn. Maybe you have your own set of sadness, Mistress, but you do not know the first thing about ours." Claudia and Annie stood beside the rock-filled coffin. Annie's arms were around her daughter's shoulders and Claudia shook but did not cry.

I stared at Lorita's wild hair, pulled back with a bandana, her massive hands and long fingernails. "Yes, you are right. I have my own set of sadness. And I know nothing of yours."

The Bible was a boulder in my hands. I thought of Jonathan, probably slapping his knees and laughing on his father's porch. If I hadn't taken Jonathan as a husband, Claudia wouldn't be going through this right now. I had no choice but to marry him. No choice but death. The thought crawled inside me like a worm.

The Swamp Sirens

Out, over the swamp, on the thickest, lowest branch of the tallest tree, they gathered. The four of them sat in a row, legs touching, and swung their feet out in front of them, trying to touch the branch above them with the tips of their lace-up boots. Each one wore the same dress, a faded yellow pinafore, with torn stockings covering four pairs of legs—two white pair, two black pair. Each one wore a yellow hair ribbon, tied in a bow on the back of her head. They hummed softly, or maybe clicked their tongues against the roof of their mouths.

"There's a croc," said Number One.

"Alligator, silly," said Number Three.

"Same difference," said Number One.

"Not if you ask the crocodiles," said Number Three.

They smiled at each other, stuck their tongues out, and resumed swinging their legs. The brush was thick in this part of the swamp. They couldn't see the big house anymore, just the beginning of the slave shacks, scattered in uneven rows, closer to the rice fields. The white woman who controlled the plantation walked through the sandy paths in a pink-feathered hat. She spoke quietly to a Negro woman who walked beside her, holding a pitcher of water. The Negro woman nodded, kissed the white woman on the cheek, and left her.

"She's coming toward the swamp," said Number Two.

"She sees us!" said Number Three.

"She can't see us," said Number Four.

"She's always seen us," said Number One.

They stood up, quickly, in the tree, and held on to higher branches with their hands. The woman in the pink-feathered hat was in a hurry. She was too dressed up for the afternoon on a weekday. She usually worked in the garden at this time. Sometimes she sat on the porch and drank lemonade, but not often.

They watched the woman pick up her pace.

"Almost as fast as a horse!" whispered Number One.

The woods buzzed. The woman kept walking. She should be careful. Her husband will be back soon. She shouldn't be walking away from the house. Everyone remembered what happened the last time she was away from the house.

"Go back!" shouted Number Two.

The woman stopped and looked around her. She could not see the tops of the tallest pines. She thought she must be imagining things. After all, she was about to do something extraordinary. The gray sand on the road had been packed flat by wagon wheels. She hardly stirred the dust when she walked. She had wanted to stop to see Faith, but she knew she couldn't. It would be too dangerous for Faith later if she were to get caught. She began walking again. The swamp was in clear view now, a huge black mouth. The opening to a tremendous other world filled with creatures that swam and slithered and slinked. Creatures that bit and pinched and strangled. The swamp was still, the odor from it a mixture of excrement and chlorophyll and salt. It was so still, she thought for a moment she could walk on it and it would hold her up.

"The alligator!" said Number One.

"Is she coming to find us?" asked Number Three.

At the edge of the swamp, the woman stood tall. She heard whisperings out over the water. They're here too, she thought. Comin' for to carry me home. She saw a stockinged leg up in the biggest tree. Heard noises. She knew they'd be here. All her life they'd been there. She played with them when she was a girl, up in the trees, deep in the forest, away from the big house and the rice fields. They took her in as one of their own, taught her how to jump from branch to branch and how to land quiet as death on the earth. When she was smaller, she understood them in some way. Or perhaps she just accepted that four girls could live in the trees, scavenging for food at night that they never seemed to eat, speaking always in short sentences, content with one another as family. As she grew older, she saw them less, thought of them more. It wasn't that uncommon for children to be left to fend for themselves. The unusual part was that two of the girls were black and two were white. She had often wondered why no one else ever seemed to see them. They giggled at her. She heard them clearly.

"Come on, Roberta!" shouted Number Three.

"Play with us!"

"Yes! We missed you!"

Roberta smiled and with the utmost precision began to unbutton her dress. She started at the high collar, sliding mother-of-pearl buttons through the eyelets. She stepped out of her dress, and paused, in her chemise and undergarments. Her skin drank the air. She knelt, allowing the mud to spread across her gray petticoat. She sat, the coolness from the damp earth shivering up her spine. She unbuttoned her shoes, and placed them side by side, facing the swamp. She pulled off her stockings and rolled them into a ball and threw them into the water. She took off her pink-feathered hat, unpinned her hair and let it flow down her back. She put the hat back on and stood. Now, she slipped off her underthings and, naked, skin bumping, hair tickling her back like a thousand fingertips, inhaled deeply and walked into the swamp.

"What's she doing?"

"Where's she going?"

"She's going to drown!"

"She's looking for us!"

"There's the alligator!"

"It's a snake."

"Watch! Watch!"

They watched and she sank deeper and deeper into the mouth of the swamp. They're calling me, she thought, right before the water moccasin slipped between her breasts and sunk its fangs into her throat. Here I come.

They watched the hat float off her head and spin counterclockwise toward the Atlantic. The alligator moved, its eyes and nostrils above the surface of the water. It swam toward the place she had been and sank into the swamp.

The four girls joined hands, sat on the largest branch of the tallest tree, leg to leg, and swung their feet out in front of them, trying to touch the branch above them with the tips of their lace-up boots.

"She's not coming back up," said Number Three.

"Nope," said Number Two.

"What'd she do that for?" asked Number One.

"Just look out there," said Number Four. "What else could she do?"

The branch above them cracked and bent. They screamed.

"It's her!" said Number One.

"Impossible," said Number Two.

"Absolutely impossible," said Number Three.

Number Four watched the branch above them, and saw just the flicker of a bare heel, swinging back and forth, dripping swamp water onto the leaves below.

Roberta du Bois

The water stuck to my body like a second skin. I pushed my whole body against the force of the water. It pushed back. After a few steps, I couldn't move my legs anymore. My feet had become stuck in the mud. A water moccasin swam beside me. I saw the outline of his diamond head pass by. The "s" shape of his path rippled in front of me like a web. I thought I should be frightened, was surprised I wasn't. I let my body fall forward into the brown liquid, my feet rooted in the marsh. My hat left my head as I sank into the swamp. The snakes came. They twisted and slapped around my legs. The bite on my calf was remarkably painless, simply an itch that was too inconvenient to scratch. I sank deeper and deeper, the water warming to my skin, or perhaps my skin cooling to the water. I didn't feel the bite on my neck. I wrapped the blanket of heavy liquid around me and drank it in. Cool, cool water.

Anything you've ever heard about the moment of death is a lie. It's been seven generations, and still I am here in the swamp. Only I'm not cold anymore, and I'm not hungry anymore. I am lonely, but given the same cards to play, I'd drink the water in again. I'd swallow the snakes, slippery and cool, until they chewed through my skin to get out.

9
The Christmas Fable

Lillian Green
1975

Mother always said folks who see things in the dark that aren't there have a touch of the devil in them. Would you say that about me, Gabriel? I'll bet you would.

Eenie meenie miney mo,
Catch a nigger by the toe.

Ever since that night in the woods I have seen the eyes. One pair, two pair, three pair. Most are brown eyes. One pair's bright blue. They watch me like they're just waiting for me to do something terrible. I tried to hide from them. No one is marching old Lillian Green off to the loony bin at this late date. But I still see them. Hear their voices sometimes too. I tell myself I'm just hearing the wind in the marsh grass or the cries of a pelican from clear down by the ocean. But I know better.

If he hollers, let him go.
Eenie meenie miney mo.

The eyes are getting brighter.

My Hannah's beautiful you know. Bright red hair. She calls it auburn, but it's red. I'm her mother. I should know. She's all grown up now, almost eighteen, but she still lives with me here, between the creeks, on this land our family has owned since—well, since always.

Hannah throws in my face everything I want to forget. She makes the voices come back. She makes the eyes sparkle in my darkness. She opens her mouth and sings like the world's gone and stopped. She can silence a room with a single note. I'm sure that's how she found you, Gabriel. She found your spirit in the woods down by the black church and she's brought you into my house. She brought you back, wrapped up nicely like a gift, and made me look at you. Made me look at everything. And then she wants me to talk about it. She doesn't know what she's asking. She doesn't know the peace that comes from not knowing.

You going to just keep staring at me? Where's Roberta? I don't know how to talk to you.

Fine.

The first thing I remember about this whole mess is the quilt. One morning I saw Mother putting some blankets into the linen closet. The one on top was so old the edges were frayed and some of the squares had pulled away from the backing, leaving a torn web of white cotton.

"Your great-great grandmother's," she said, stuffing the quilt up on the highest shelf out of my reach. "Great-great grandma Faith."

I imagine I was close to nine years old. "I don't remember seeing that before."

I'll never forget. Mother looked at me like I was wearing socks on my hands and said, "It's best this way." I went back downstairs and began to play with my paper dolls.

I didn't really think about the quilt again until that night my brother went crazy and I took it apart to stuff its insides down my throat.

I come to you now an old woman, Gabriel. I never thought I'd be in this place, standing here in front of you with my hands open. Gabriel, look at me. Here I am at the end of my life and there is only this quilt between us and my daughter's sweet sweet voice. Just you and me and all the things that have been.

Look, Gabriel. My hands are open.

Lillian Green
1972

I held my gin and tonic in my right hand, enjoying the cool feel of the glass against my palm. Hannah was in her room listening to the radio too loud. No moon cut a light across the living room floor. I had changed into my house dress, my favorite one with the dark green velvet trim around the sleeves. This last part of the evening when civilized people were awake was my time for talk. The gin helped me loosen my throat, helped me forget I was in my living room, alone, preparing for conversation. Helped me forget no one but the mail carrier ventured up my driveway anymore.

I like to think Roberta enjoyed these times too. After all, no one came to visit her either, or so I reckoned. She didn't speak much. I did most of the talking, confessing, lamenting of the evening. She was kind enough to sit across from me, straight back, hands folded on her lap, and nod from time to time. Her biggest kindness was coming at all to be with me—almost a real companion. I felt no judgment from her as she sat across from me, the occasional snake hanging from her hat. We were wounded in the same way.

Every once in awhile, especially when the snake was awake, she'd speak of it. "Sometimes I can't believe what a body can bear."

I thought of Gabriel Wilson, as I always did, and tried to conjure up what he would have been like alive. Not the little bit of alive he was when I saw him, but alive enough to go fishing, to dance with his sister, to get on his knees to be closer to God.

"See that tree over there in the water?" She pointed out the window. She knew I knew the tree, even though it was too dark to see.

The swamp had a grove of moss-laden trees growing in it. The center tree was bigger around than a doublewide and it wore its moss like a jacket. "That tree didn't used to be in the water so much. The ground there was always sinking a little when you walked on it, but it hadn't been swallowed by the swamp then. It's like the swamp hadn't been fed enough yet. We buried the box of rocks out under that tree, and it's true, the ground was so soft all you really had to do was set the coffin on the earth and in a few hours the earth would swallow it. Nobody'd ever have to know what was done out there under that tree."

"What box of rocks?" I asked.

"A baby," she whispered. "Faith." She stood and the snake opened its jaws, the white cotton of its mouth a web. "Doesn't matter. It was just one more time I didn't do enough."

"How do you know what enough is?" My drink was empty, but I didn't want to move to refill it.

"Maybe enough is when you don't feel guilty anymore for what you don't do. Maybe there is no 'enough.' Maybe we're supposed to feel guilty. Maybe the most dangerous person is someone who doesn't."

I heard Hannah's bedroom door open. "She thinks I'm terrible," I said.

Roberta smiled. "But she has no idea why, does she? Why are you terrible?"

"I got frozen," I said. "I just got frozen."

She made a step towards me, then stopped. "That's what the water's for, honey. It helps you melt a little."

"Who are you talking to, Mother?" Hannah, red hair wild around her head, Mickey Mouse sleeping shirt around her body, stood in front of us. But there was no us, just me. She looked at my empty glass.

"Just the house, sweetie. Just talking to the house."

She didn't believe me, as usual, and huffed back to her room. I poured another drink and thought about Roberta's box of rocks and why the water can't seem to keep down what it's been fed.

Dear Mommy,

Where is my daddy? Emily Peterson at school says my daddy is a no 'count. I don't know how she knows that, but she seems real certain. I hit her over the head with my math book when no one was looking. She didn't tell on me either. Must mean she knew she was telling stories.

I sure wish I had known a story to tell back to her. Maybe I walk past daddy all the time on my way to school and don't recognize him. Do you think that could be right, Mama? Do you?

Love,
Hannah
Age 10

Lillian Green
1968

She asks about you, Jay. All the other little girls have daddies and she wonders why it is she doesn't have one. She thinks you know about her. I've read her letters, but I don't know how to answer. She thinks you're choosing to stay away from her. I guess in a way you are choosing to stay away from her. Sometimes I do want to tell you. I want to track you down somehow and let you know what-all you're missing. But I can't seem to quite get past that leap of forgiveness to do all that for you. I can't quite get past the sound of the gravel from your own car tires as you drove away. Can't get past the moment when I gave you all the cards and saw all you could do was fold like a yellow dog. Just fold. I can't forgive you for that. Not in this life. Not in the next one either. You remember that, Jay Transom, if you ever darken my door again, it was you who folded, not me. Not me.

Lillian Green
1974

I entered the day room at Charlotte State Hospital and saw Tommy sitting in front of the window watching a cardinal struggling, lodged between the rusted bars covering the window. The bird's neck was bent precariously and it beat against the iron with its one free wing. The flapping was furious for a few moments, then paused, then resumed, then paused. Soon it would stop. Tommy didn't move. Didn't hear me come in. The bird's blood was deeper crimson than its feathers.

"Tommy?" I pulled one of the lime-green metal folding chairs over beside him and sat down. I put my hands on his knees. When I looked at him like this, face to face, I always thought of bears or old miners—men with crusty faces and yellowed teeth. Tommy had both, and the strong, tall build of a grizzly bear. I put my hand on his thick shoulder. He jerked, startled, the veins in his neck popping blue under his skin. "It's me, Tommy. Don't be frightened. It's Lillian."

He smiled at me, pointed at the bird, then smashed his eyes with his fists, a game he played when he wanted not to be seen. "Dead bird."

"Not yet, Tommy." I looked at the struggling cardinal. "Soon."

I opened my purse. "I brought you a present."

He held out his hands, palms up, to receive it.

"I made it myself. I thought you could put it in your room."

I placed the heart-shaped cross-stitched pillow in his hands. It had taken me the better part of a month to make all the tiny stitches. It read "Jesus Loves Me" in one-inch gold-thread letters and there was a cross in the background made out of three shades of red thread. The first letter of each word was slightly larger than the rest and was highlighted with a single strand of emerald green thread. The jutting shape of the hill of Golgotha was made of black thread, tiny knots accentuating each angle of the mountain. The back of the pillow was burgundy velvet. I thought it might be soothing for him to touch. I was going to put lace around the edges to add a softer element, but something about frilly lace framing a crucifixion scene didn't seem right. It was more the words I was going for anyway. I wanted Tommy to believe someone loved him. Even if I wasn't so sure.

He took the pillow and pressed it to his face. "Fab," he said. He'd taken lately to identifying things by the detergent they were washed in.

"Yes, honey. Fab. Do you know what it says?"

He pointed to the cross. "Jesus."

I nodded. "What else?"

"I can read."

"I know you can."

The bird let out a cry I was surprised to hear through the glass.

"Dead," said Tommy.

"Not yet." Another cardinal had arrived, hearing the cries, perhaps, and crashed into the glass. Its beak, bent; wings trapped between the bars and the glass. Both birds now struggled.

He held the pillow inches from his face. "Loves me."

"That's right. Who loves you?"

"You!" He smiled big and wide like the Tommy I remembered from forty years ago. Smiled like the Tommy I wanted him to be. I reached back into my purse to pull out a tissue, and when I glanced back up, Tommy had ripped the backing off the pillow. He pulled the stuffing out in handfuls. "For the birds' nests," he said, pointing at the cardinals.

"Tommy, honey, don't do that." I wanted to yank that pillow out of his hands, but I didn't dare. I knew it would cause a tantrum that would require the floor nurse. The last time I tried to keep

Tommy from doing something, he raged, stomping the picnic lunch I'd brought from Hardee's into a greasy lump on the floor. Because of that incident, outside food was no longer allowed in the ward. I pressed my lips together. The cardinals pecked at each other.

Tommy spread the stuffing on the floor around his chair. "It's snowing!" He laid his hands over the layer of white cotton fluff as if he were laying hands on a wounded child. "Just like Christmas!" The television droned "The Price is Right".

"It is almost Christmas," I said, trying to gather up the stuffing from the cold floor.

"Mother coming for Christmas?" Tommy made trails in the stuffing with his fingers. I touched the back of his hand.

"Mother died, honey. You remember? You wore that beautiful suit that the staff got for you special."

"You can still go to the Christmas pageant at church even if Mother died, right?"

He giggled, a half-laugh that caught in his throat, and he began to unravel the stitching on my pillow with his teeth.

"You want me to go to the Christmas pageant?" I hadn't been back in church since Mother's funeral.

Tommy nodded furiously. "I was a wise man."

The last time Tommy had gone to church with us, both of us had been in the pageant. He indeed had been a wise man. I was an angel.

"Go. Take pictures!" He smiled and continued to pull, one stitch at a time until he had a pile of wet, red thread in his lap, the end still in his mouth. "Love you, Butter Bean," he said, arranging the string in his mouth with his tongue.

I pulled him closer to me so he could rest his head on my shoulder, the pile of string a life rope between us. I closed my eyes. Tommy, washing his truck, squirting me with the garden hose. Tommy, helping Mother and me hang the heavy draperies in the living room. Tommy, teasing me and my girlfriends on the way to school. Tommy, tossing a rope over a tree. "Love you back." I said, and left him sitting by the window.

Outside, the cardinals' battle was waning. The bird that had been trapped the longest was dead. Its black eye looked like hematite. Its skull was the size of both my thumbs. Three feathers were pulled backwards, away from the others, trapped in the bars. The living bird's body was keeping the dead one's from sliding to the ground, its single free wing beating steadily against the glass.

February 14, 1968

Dear Daddy,

I thought I would write a letter to you on Valentine's Day. Lots of girls in my class get chocolate from their daddies on Valentine's Day. Mama won't tell me anything about you except that you sang, too. Is that why she doesn't like my voice? Does it sound like yours? I wonder if we would be friends. I like to think so. I like to pretend sometimes, when only the woman in the pink feathered hat is nearby, that you and I are singing a duet somewhere together and everybody is clapping. Even Mama.

Sincerely,
Your Daughter
Hannah Green

Lillian Green
1974

I went to the annual church Christmas pageant at Cornerstone Southern Baptist Church because Tommy asked me to. Although that was several weeks ago, and Tommy no doubt no longer remembered asking me, I felt duty-bound to show up and at least pick up a program.

When I walked into the sanctuary, I was nearly run over by one of the little Mullen boys who was sobbing, wearing a pink bed sheet on his head. "Sorry, Miss Green," he said, wiped his nose, adjusted his headdress, and hurried up to the front of the church. I quickly scanned the aisle for any more runaway shepherds. God rest ye merry gentlemen, I thought, adjusting my own red hat, complete with the requisite green and gold holly berry decoration adorning the brim. The hat smelled a little funny, moldy, like when I forget to empty out the Tupperware in the refrigerator.

"Lillian! Welcome!" I found myself in the huge, squishy embrace of Mrs. Robertson Chatlin, the choir director. "So nice to see you here again. We've missed you!"

"Mrs. Chatlin. How wonderful to see you, too. Seems like you have a very active group again this year."

"Every year! The little dears! I just love when they say 'Behold! I bring you great news!' and sing 'Away in the Manger.'" She released me and pressed her right hand against her heart. "It gets me." She tapped her chest with blood-red manicured nails. "Right here."

"Mrs. Chatlin!" A host of hallowed angels had suddenly materialized behind her, tugging at her dress. "Mrs. Chatlin! Donny spilled cherry Kool-Aid on the baby Jesus!"

Mrs. Chatlin smiled, crimson lipstick on her coffee stained teeth. "My work is never done!" And she whirled away like the tornado that carried Dorothy to Oz. I once again adjusted my hat; the smell of the Love's Baby Soft Mrs. Chatlin had sponge bathed in strong in my nostrils. I took a deep breath. Christmas comes but once a year. I was here for Tommy. If I had my way, I'd be back at home wrapped up in my quilt.

The stairs to the basement where the big show took place were just to the right of the greeters. With any luck, I could make it downstairs and begin mingling before anyone noticed I had not brought a covered dish.

I heard the children loudly shushing each other in the hall that ran parallel to the chapel. When Tommy was a Wise Man, his line was, "We bring you frankincense and Myrrh, O King." I was part of the heavenly host and wore wings made of chicken wire and cotton balls. The first hint of stubble had begun to show on Tommy's chin. Sheriff Paterson, the same man who one year later would come to our house after Gabriel was found and strike a deal with Daddy behind closed doors to keep Tommy out of prison, also served as deacon, and was the main announcer for the program that evening. I remember thinking that without his Sheriff's hat, he looked like he could have been playing one of the Wise Men. I believed then. Not so much the story—the Virgin birth, the journey to Bethlehem, the visit from the angels—but I believed in the redemption. The forgiveness of sins, the resurrection of the body and thelifeeverlasting-amen. These things, for a time, I was sure of.

My footsteps echoed in the stairwell on the way down to the basement. The long metal tables covered in green paper tablecloths were filling up with baked hams, orange Jell-O salad with marshmallows, and string beans cooked in bacon grease and salt water. I smiled at Mrs. Linston, my old third-grade teacher who now used a walker and talked loudly to her dead husband when she waited in the cashier's line at Luby's Cafeteria. I waved and blew a kiss at Mrs. Johnson and her scandalous live-in Jake, and I mouthed the obligatory "you must come over and see me sometime" to the Bensons and their seven sticky-faced children. The south end of the basement was decorated with hundreds of poinsettias in green and red wrapped pots. I seemed to recall poinsettias were poisonous to cats and I thought of releasing a dozen cats into the room on the promise of all-you-can-eat marshmallow Jell-O just to see what miracles the precious Jesus could pull off these days.

Three tables lined the west wall, covered with devil's food cakes dripping with extra fudge, spongy angel food cakes covered with canned peaches, plate after plate of fried chicken, including a bucket straight from Kentucky Fried. Had to be Mrs. Peterson's. Anyone else would have at least taken it out of the bucket and put it on their nicest plate. Green plastic forks and spoons stuck out of the main dishes like meat thermometers. Someone had brought Swedish meatballs dipped in tomato sauce. Tiny rectangles of green peppers floated in the paste. A cherry ham rimmed with candied apples had the place of prominence on the middle table.

The only place left to sit was by the radiator. A family of three I didn't know sat along the far edge of that table. They would probably leave me alone. I picked up a paper plate decorated with silver bells and thumped two Swedish meatballs onto it. I was about to scoop some of the fudge from the devil's food cake with my finger when the organist began. Three chords—Gs—in a row. The laughing and talking stopped. The shouts of "Merry Christmas" fell to the white tiled floor.

"Welcome ya'll," said the Sheriff, adjusting his red bow tie with his right hand. "So glad to see so many of you out here on this very exciting Christmas week! As you know, the children have been preparing all month for this special event, so without further delay, let me present 'A Christmas Story', by the youth of Cornerstone Southern Baptist Church!"

We'd have applauded if it was allowed, but since God didn't care for foolishness in his house, even in his basement, we smiled as broadly as we could and scratched our collective itches while sheep, donkeys, lowing cattle and the occasional shepherd paraded in two-by-two like refugees from Noah's ark. A little boy with perfect golden curls came to the front and cleared his little boy throat three times before beginning, screaming at the top of his lungs, "This is a story of GOOD NEWS! The GOOD NEWS of the birth of our Savior, Jesus Christ, in humble beginnings in a stable in Bethlehem." He waved to a woman the front row who whispered loud enough to be heard in the Methodist church, "I love you, honey!"

"I love you, Butter Bean."

Tommy. My Wise Man.

We were plunged into darkness and an old spotlight borrowed from the high school shone on a cardboard manger, where the perfect family smiled in too-tight costumes directly into the blinding light.

10
Opportunities

Roberta du Bois

I had a chance to kill Jonathan. Every wife always has that chance. It'd be dishonest of me now and in this place to tell you otherwise. Every time a man drinks too much and falls asleep, there's that chance.

The night I almost did it had only a sliver of a moon. We had just buried the box of rocks for Claudia. Jonathan had just bought another woman. A young one. She hadn't stopped crying since she got to us, two days before. Nobody would talk to her. She screamed like she was crazy. She wasn't crazy. Just sixteen years old and far far away from anybody's loving arms. Far far away from any rest.

"She says her name's Esther," Jonathan said at supper that night.

I set down my crystal water glass. "Where did she come from?"

"Louisiana."

"Esther's a strange name for Louisiana folks."

"Well, you know how they are."

"Mmm."

I knew he wanted someone to replace Claudia. This woman, Esther, already had four teeth gone, never coming back. Already had arm muscles twice as big as my own and eyes I knew had seen things they never could stop seeing.

Jonathan pushed back from the table, wobbling. "Think I'll turn in early."

"Mmm."

When he left the room, I realized I'd been holding my breath. The corset pulled my ribcage together, making it impossible to let all my breath go. I scraped the leftover food from his plate onto my own and began stacking the dishes. Claudia heard and came in to take away the linens. "Her name not Esther," she said. "Her name Sawanee, like the river."

If Jonathan were to die, not one person would mourn. I was sure of it. I couldn't bring myself to have empathy for his mama and daddy; all I could see was freedom dancing all around me. I took a carving knife from the table.

"Don't do that, Miss," said Claudia. "He ain't worth it."

"You're right about that," I said. "He's not worth a thing."

"They'll get you for it, Miss. You know they will."

I did. I'd probably get put in an asylum. Lots of women go mad. No one pays too much attention.

"What about us, Miss, if they get you?" Claudia couldn't look up at me. She held the tablecloth close.

I walked away from her, the weight of the knife comfortable in my hand. But even as I walked with it, I knew I wouldn't do it. Claudia was right. What would happen to her? I didn't have to ask. Still, I walked up the stairs into our bedroom, where Jonathan hadn't even removed his boots before collapsing on the velvet coverlet. I just wanted to feel the possibility. I imagined the back of the blade might feel like ice chips on his neck. I imagined he'd roll into the knife, grateful for the cool water. I imagined when he realized it was me, he'd tip his hat, even laugh a little at being undone by a woman. I imagined he'd bleed out quickly, like a hog, and we could clean it up and bury him in the swamp, maybe wrapped in a linen tablecloth.

But it was just imagining. Instead, I pulled his muddy boots off one by one. I hefted his legs up onto the bed, even straightened out his head so he wouldn't get a kink.

It was the human thing to do.

11
Of Bats and Wings

May 23, 1976

Dear Mama,

Just thought I'd tell you I'm going to try my hand at writing songs. I've been writing poetry for a long time now and it just feels right. Maybe if I quit doing so many cover tunes and do some of my own stuff I might be able to get famous and go to New York. I've been playing out here by the Cape Fear River on weekends, trying to save up some money for a bus ticket north. It's hard to have people walk by and not pay any attention, but I guess I am pretty used to that. That's one thing you taught me, Mama. How to be ignored.

They do clap for me, Mama. Especially after a Bessie Smith song and if the tugboats haven't been too loud behind me. People stop their cars and listen to me.

They really do clap for me.

Love,
Hannah
Age 17

Hannah Green
1976

Writing music isn't as easy as I thought it would be. I figured you get a few chords going and just open up your lungs and the words would come. Not so. Least not for me yet. But I'm working on it. My first album will be an entire compilation of originals. It'll be called *Hannah: True Blue* and the cover art will be pieces from Picasso's blue period and will create an ocean effect from the geometric shapes. I can see it perfectly in my head. Kind of like I can hear the words I want to write in my head, but when I go to actually put them on the paper, they pull a disappearing act. I'm going to have to find a way to corral them like sheep instead of cats.

I like to think about what my first reviews will say. I am the white woman with the voice of Aretha Franklin. I shake like Elvis. Mourn like Etta James. Folks'll say, "How does a girl that young know the blues?" I'll give a faraway look, toss my hair, and smile like a movie star. I can't be categorized. I like it that way. I don't know where my voice comes from. I don't know why I feel the rhythms in a different way from Mama. It's part of the reason Mama won't come hear me sing. But God help us if she'd ever offer up any information. Mama would be a great prisoner of war. The code of silence she upholds is unbreakable.

Maybe I should write a song about the people in the walls or Mama's silence. That might be better. It's what I know, and that's what they say, right? Write what you know. What would I say without sounding stupid? I saw the wallpaper move when I was three and my world turned upside down? What kind of song would that be?

Dear Mama,

I wrote my first song about you, and when I played it down on the boardwalk, I made a whole ten dollars. You should have come see me. Guess lots of people can connect to abandonment. I had a great high note in there too— just like the ones you wouldn't let me make in church. I hit 'em good, Mama. Good and long, and no one would know I was not even eighteen. No one would know I was all alone.

Except maybe they would. It's hard to hide the lonely when you sing.

Your Daughter,
Hannah

Lillian Green
1976

I snuck out to follow Hannah after she left the house for her gig at the Cape Fear River. It was the first time I'd snuck anywhere since 1949. Most times, it was easier for us to just pass each other in the hall. I knew, Lord knows I knew, how good her voice was. And Lord knows I knew where she got it from. I wanted to take back how I'd treated her that day in church when she sang. I wanted to pull that day back inside me like a ball of twine and let her have her moment without my shame coating her with its tar. Or, if it had to come out and darken her too, at least I could tell her why—what it was and where it came from—and most importantly, tell her she didn't have to take on all our grown-up mess if she didn't want to. Times were changing fast. It wasn't 1957 anymore. It wasn't 1949 anymore. Civil rights had come even to Alderman, at least on the surface. The signs for whites and coloreds were gone. Anybody could sit anyplace on the bus. But just because things are different out in the open doesn't mean anything had changed at all beneath the surface.

All I seemed to be able to do now was dress up like someone who might be comfortable going out walking by the river at night by herself and to hide in the shadows and hope that being proud of her from a distance would amount to more than not being proud of her at all.

I wore a deep blue dress that had fit me once, but now clung to parts of my back and thighs I hadn't quite noticed had grown so much. I wrapped a black crocheted shawl around my shoulders, traced my lips in beige, and drove to the waterfront. My feet were uncertain on the gravel parking lot, even in the 1-1/2" sling back heels. The humidity, or my nervousness, caused my pantyhose to stick to my legs.

The waterfront smelled like wet tennis shoes. I wished I had left my purse safe in the trunk of the car. Everyone seemed to be smoking while they window-shopped or watched the water. I couldn't take in a good breath.

Hannah's hair seemed on fire through the scrim of orange streetlights and cigarette smoke. She needed no microphone. Her arms were covered in silver bangles I didn't remember seeing before. Her white skin shone against the black dress, which fit her as I remembered my blue dress used to fit me. But I didn't remember that I could ever move like she could in it. Her hips moved like they weren't attached to her spine. Each hip must have been connected to a marionette string held somewhere high above her. Her arms were snakes, cutting the smoky air into spirals. She sang Ida Cox's "Graveyard Dream Blues."

I went to the graveyard
fell down on my knees

She could have stepped out of 1920 right into that piece of music. Just like that, she stepped out of herself into the gospel and right back into the blues. She didn't just sing; she became the notes. I saw them swimming around her, treble clefs and bass clefs, quarter notes, half notes, dancing right along with her snaky arms. For a moment, I imagined her arm snakes found me, slithered right on across the dance floor, up under the soles of my too-high-for-my-taste shoes and up around my shoulders. Hugging me.

Tugboats moved slowly behind her. A black storm approached from the Atlantic, but she didn't notice, she was so caught up in song. People stopped walking and listened to her. Really listened, cigarettes glowing beside their cheeks.

Hannah's snakes shook me in the center of the woman I used to be. They shook me up into my intestines and into my lungs and flew out my surprisingly open mouth back into the smoke, back to my daughter. My beautiful baby. She sang me awake for a long enough moment to forget my purse, forget my age, forget my sorrows. She sang me awake long enough to dance, all by myself on the boardwalk along the ancient Cape Fear River, pantyhose bunched behind my kneecaps.

My goodness, can my baby sing.

Hannah Green
1976

I was singing up at the river when he walked up to me. It was a Wednesday night, so there weren't too many folks out. Mama stayed away, as always. This was one of those nights when there was just me and the smoke and the tugboats. I'd just finished an old Etta James tune, when he moved close enough to make me stop. He wore a ragged pair of Reeboks. His Levis were faded at the knees. I'd never seen him before. Alderman isn't the biggest city in the world, and I've lived here my whole life. If Mama and I don't know someone, they're a stranger. We might not have any friends, but we know everybody. That's what a small town is.

"I'm Hannah," I said, and held out my hand to him.

He took my hand. "Hello, Hannah."

"You're new here."

"Not really." He released my hand. "I used to hang around here all the time. Back when you must have been a little bitty baby."

I bristled. "I'm not as young as you think."

"Neither am I."

"Well, I hope you're enjoying the show."

"Just got here, so it's kind of hard to tell. My name is Jay."

"Nice to meet you, Jay." A policeman was on his way over. I'm supposed to have a permit to sing here. They don't usually bother me when I'm actually singing, though. "I have to go back to work." The cop was almost within earshot. "Gotta go."

He nodded and backed away.

"Welcome back, everybody," I said to nobody but Jay and the

policeman. "Hope you enjoyed the break. Now, I'd like to bring it back down with a little Lena Horne number."

Jay pulled out a tiny spiral notebook from his shirt pocket and flipped open the cover. Who was this guy?

I cleared my throat and began to hum, then held my head up, and raised my arms to the night sky as I released the notes I always carry with me.

He handed me his business card after it got too cold to play.

Jay Transom, Producer, Gecko Records, New York City, and the phone number. The card was on off-white stock with forest-green lettering, and a yellow lizard curled in the upper right corner.

"Interesting company name," I said. "Don't think I've ever heard of it."

He tapped his knuckles on the vinyl tablecloth. "Don't imagine you would down here. We mainly work with New Yorkers. Kinda work the art scene, you know?"

"You don't sound like you're from New York. You sound like you're from right around the corner."

Jay's lips twisted before he lied. "I guess I just blend in wherever I go. Like a gecko."

I sat down with him anyway, even though I knew geckos didn't change colors, chameleons did. Thank you Mrs. Simpson's Life Science class. "You sure you don't have people around here?"

His eyes darkened a minute. "I'm sure."

"So, I could use some coffee." I'd just started drinking coffee a few months ago and it still felt crazy-grown-up.

"I already ordered one for you."

I took him in. Ragged Levis. Dirty boots. Pockmarked face covered with salt and pepper facial hair. His eyes were hazel, beneath black lashes. "No cream or sugar. Just black."

His lips twitched. "Just black."

I laughed. "OK, Mr. Jay Transom, of Gecko Records, New York City. What brings you to this boardwalk on this night, and what on earth are you doing talking to me?"

"Would you believe Diana Ross stood me up and I had nowhere else to go?"

I shook my head. He was watching my hair. They always did. I'm not sure where it comes from. My mother has fine, limp hair that she bleaches more than her sheets. Mine is like a shampoo commercial. Truly. It always gets attention.

"Your hair is beautiful," he said.

I pulled some strands of hair through my fingers and twirled the ends. "This is what I've got. Hair and lungs."

"I'll say yes to both. Your voice is amazing."

"So then, do you sing too?"

He stroked his chin. "Used to. Not so much anymore. Spending more time recruiting the talent, you know? Man's gotta make a living."

"So you're here as a talent scout?" I smiled my most perfect $1000-worth-of-dental-work smile. This was my big break out of here.

"I'm just here to relax," he said. "Take in some good music. Chat with the locals."

I wasn't going to get too hopeful. "Well, Mr. Transom, I hope you've enjoyed your chat with the locals. I best be getting home."

He reached for my arm. "Can I walk you to your car?"

I knew enough to know that wasn't appropriate. "I don't think so. You stay and finish your coffee. Maybe I'll see you around sometime." I always wanted to say that line. It was good practice for when I'm famous and doing interviews with *Rolling Stone.*

"I hope so," he said. "Good night, Hannah."

"Good night, Jay."

When I got safely inside the car, I let it rip. An agent! He was an agent! I, Hannah Green, just met an agent! I was too excited to even start the car. In my mind, I was already in New York making a record with Sony. I was already far far away from Mama and all the people in the walls. I always knew this was going to happen, even if Mama never believed. I always knew.

Dear Mama,

I met a man tonight who seemed kind of interesting. He wrote stuff down while I was singing, and he stayed for the entire set. I think you will like him. He's an agent and he thinks I can make it in New York. He said I'm "fresh" and that he'd never heard anybody sing quite like me, not even Janis Joplin. What do you think of that, Mama? Not even Janis Joplin. Of course, I'm not going to be stupid, but I'm also not going to risk my big break. I've been trying to get away from here my whole life. It's a shame you never heard me sing. It's a shame you never thought I could do it. Because I'm going to, Mama. I'm going to go to New York with this man and I'm going to be a star. The biggest brightest star you've ever seen. Maybe you'll come listen to me when I'm on Broadway. You'll have to call ahead to see if I can get you tickets.

Anyway, now that I'm eighteen, you can't say no, but I'll bring him by in a few days so you can meet him so you won't be scared.

Sincerely,
H

Dear Mama,

I just wanted to say good-bye. I've been packing. I'll leave most everything and take just the essentials. I don't know what else to say.

Dear Mama,

I'm leaving tomorrow for New York and I

Dear Mama,

Funny how I have no words anymore after all this time of writing to you. I wish you'd read my letters. I wish you'd have talked to me. I wish a lot.
Mommy,
I'm sorry you're so alone.

Love,
Hannah

Lillian Green
1976

When I saw Jay walk in my own front door with my only daughter, my mouth went dry as fur. I had pictured him coming back for close to twenty years, but never like this. He knew before I knew. He must have recognized the house. I may not have kept it up as nice as Mama, but I knew he could never forget the land. The acres of pines we walked through. The porch where we first kissed. The gravel driveway where he drove away. What must he have thought, driving up that hill again with Hannah?

He was still beautiful. Hazel eyes framed with black lashes. Was it really almost twenty years ago? Upstairs in this house on the bed I still sleep in is where he pressed his tongue against the freckle on my arm. Upstairs where he drew out the first sounds of desire; where he created the first need I have never found a way to fill again.

He remembered. His arms were stiff at his sides. He wore a dirty denim jacket and Levis held around his waist with a brown belt. Hannah followed him like a puppy, flames of hair falling over her shoulders as she walked.

Into my house.

My house.

I had wrapped my head in a red scarf. It had been days since I washed my hair. He spoke first and when he did, Hannah dropped her arms and backed away, almost hitting the coat rack.

"Lillian," he said, his voice as smooth as a young Elvis, just like I remembered.

"Jay."

"Mother?" Hannah had regained her composure and attempted to link her arm with Jay's. He kept his arms straight at his sides. He didn't look at her. This was the man. Oh dear God, this was the man my little girl thought she was going to New York with. The man she thought was an agent. Maybe he was. What did I know anymore? Hannah smiled a little, just the corners of her mouth. "You two know each other?"

It was 1957 again. The sky was cloudy and two cardinals watched us from the trees. I drank a glass of lemonade, sticky as the truth.

"I thought you'd come back," I said. "I waited."

Hannah put the pieces together first. "This Jay is your Jay? Mother, this Jay is my—oh God!"

I wanted to reach for her, but felt pinned to the wall. The tea kettle whistled. We stood there, in the foyer, listening. "I better go get that," I said.

"Don't you move." Hannah stormed past me into the kitchen. "Seems like you two need to talk."

"Hannah!" Jay called to her, but she had slammed the door to the kitchen. He looked at me, once again, with the same loathing he had the day he drove away. "Is there something you need to tell me?"

I opened my mouth and made a sound like crying, but without tears, without passion.

"Don't pull this on me again." He grabbed my wrist and pulled me into the living room. Rough as he was, I wanted his fingers to stay there. If he touched me, well, if he touched me at all, he was still here. I was still here. "Don't clam all up like you've got nothing to tell me. We've been down this road before. You kept another secret from me, didn't you?"

"Jay, I—you left. You drove away and left me. You never even looked back."

"I sat at the end of the driveway until it was dark. You never came after me."

"I shouldn't have had to come after you! Besides, how would I know you sat there? The end of the driveway was a half-mile away!"

He opened his mouth but couldn't think of anything to say. Got him, smoothtalker.

"I told you what you begged me to tell you! I was the one who believed you when you said you loved me. You needed to come back for me. I was fourteen years old when I made my mistake. You were almost thirty."

He sat on the Victorian sofa, elbows on his knees. "You didn't make a mistake. You made a choice."

"So did you."

I didn't hear anything from the kitchen. Hannah was probably listening at the door. I couldn't blame her. I caught a rippling in the wallpaper from the corner of my eye.

"You didn't even tell her about me?"

"What was to tell? You bailed on me the first time things got tough. I didn't want her thinking her father was spineless."

"Do you not get it still? Even now? The man your brother killed was my family. You let it happen. You let him die."

"Talk." The brown eyes spoke from the ceiling beams.

"Shut up."

"Are you talking to me?" asked Jay.

I shook my head. "Just the voices."

He sighed. "What did you tell her about me?"

I couldn't get enough air. "I told her you were a musician. I told her I loved you. I told her you loved her."

"How many lies can a woman string together, Lillian. God, you're amazing. How do you keep it all straight?"

"Why don't you tell me? Tell me how many lies I've told you. I'm sure you've kept count. Tell me one good reason why you think telling you the truth would have been a better choice? I did that too, remember? I could have choked in the dust you left."

"She's my daughter. How dare you!"

I crossed to him. "You stop right there. I have taken responsibility all my life for what I did with Gabriel. I will even take responsibility for keeping Hannah from you, but let me ask you this. How much effort was I supposed to spend trying to find you? How much time was I supposed to spend sniffing after the man who walked out on me?"

"As much as it took to find him." Hannah stood behind me, face red and blotchy.

If there had been anything left inside me at all, I would have never stopped crying.

"Hannah," said Jay. "I didn't know. I swear it."

She nodded, turned to me. "You knew where he was."

"No, Hannah. I didn't know."

"Why did you never try to find me?" she screamed. "How could you leave me here with all these dead people everywhere?"

She walked back into the kitchen. Jay reached out his arm to her.

"Don't go after her," I said. "You have no right."

"I have every right. She is my child."

"She is my child." I pulled the scarf out of my hair and wrapped it around my fingers. "Why couldn't you forgive me? I never understood."

"I don't know." He touched my cheek with the back of his hand. "I did love you."

I cleared my throat. "Did."

He bit his lower lip. "Did."

"Alright then." I inhaled deeply. "That's that. Can I get you some water? Maybe a little tea? Staying for supper, aren't you?"

"Don't be that way."

"Don't take my anger from me. You've taken everything else."

Jay glanced at the kitchen. "So have you."

He went after her anyway. I heard her pound on his chest. Cry. I could still feel the tenderness of his hand on my face. If he had slapped me, I would have felt better. Anger could be dealt with. Apathy breaks everything. I had been here before. What could I do but open the door to the kitchen, look at them both, chess pieces from some sick game on the yellow flecked linoleum, and speak?

When I told them, Jay again, Hannah for the first time, about Tommy and Gabriel and what happened after Jay drove away into the storm, I felt as if I were floating above my body, watching myself at forty explain myself at twenty-two and at fourteen. The words made no sense out of context. The context made no sense without the words.

"Uncle Tommy murdered somebody?" asked Hannah.

"Uncle Tommy doesn't remember anymore."

"The hell he doesn't," said Jay.

"Hannah, honey, you've seen your uncle. He doesn't even know what year it is."

"Jay," she said. "Dad," she said. "I have to take a shower."

She left us alone again. When I heard the water running in the back bathroom, I tried to touch Jay's arm. He pulled away from me. "Don't."

"What are we going to do?"

"Seems like you've gotten yourself into another mess, Lillian. I'm going back to New York. Hannah can come or she can stay with you. I'll be gone by dawn."

"Just like before. I see your coping skills have matured quite nicely. Are you even an agent, or were you just trying to score some young girlfriend?"

He closed his eyes. "I never knew how much I had to regret before I met you." His hand was on the doorknob. The sounds from the shower stopped.

"Maybe she'll be down soon," I said. "Stay."

"I have to go."

"For her."

"It's getting cold up north. I don't want to get stuck in the snow."

"They have snowplows."

"I imagine they do."

Hannah came back down the stairs, blue terrycloth towel wrapped around her head. "You two haven't killed each other yet?"

"Honey," I said.

"Shut up."

"Hannah," said Jay.

"Shut up."

Hannah Green
1976

Jay/Dad agreed to stay a few days, but he might as well have gone for all the good it did us. Mama hadn't been the same after he showed up. Whatever same might mean. She didn't talk to the ghosts anymore. She left them, louder and more aggressive than ever to talk to me. Now, she didn't talk at all. At least not much talk that made any sense.

"Won't you go visit Tommy?" she said, over and over. "He used to take me to the ocean to watch the sailboats. Every Saturday morning we'd go. His eyes were blue as the ocean. Now his eyes are black. Won't you go visit him?"

I didn't answer her. Jay/Dad didn't answer her. She walked out the front door, started the car, and was gone.

"Hannah," he said, then covered his mouth with his fingers.

"What just happened?" I asked, my own fingers not knowing what to do.

He shook his head. "Another lie."

The house settled. Every crick and pop that used to bring comfort pinched my spine. This house was too big. Too many creatures lived here.

"Do you know where she is now?"

"Mama? Not a clue. She took off to see Tommy, probably." I pulled at my fingers. Bad habit I acquired in junior high.

"Mess up your knuckles that way. It'll be hard for you to play guitar."

"I know." I kept pulling on them. I saw the face of the ghost woman reflected in the picture window. "She's right there."

"Who?"

"The woman! That ghost that Mama prays to. Can't you see her?"

Jay/Dad shook his head. He looked pathetic to me. Weak. Whimpering. What kind of man would leave a pregnant woman anyway? Wouldn't a father know he had a child, even if he was never told? Isn't there supposed to be some kind of parental instinct or something? I wrote letters to him. Didn't he know?

"Get out of my house."

"Hannah, I—don't you think we should talk?"

I closed my eyes. "What's to talk about?" I waved my hand in front of my face as if I could make him disappear – go with the ghost woman. I felt sicker than I ever knew possible.

Mama appeared in the doorway. At that moment, I thought she might have materialized from the atoms. Maybe I had imagined the car driving away. "Won't you go visit Tommy?"

Jay/Dad pushed past me. Mama opened her arms to him as if she were going to embrace him, but he slapped her hands down. She whimpered. Both of them dissolved into infants. I had enough.

"You're the grown-ups!" I shrieked. "You! Both of you! Look at what your lies have done!"

Something crashed against the window. The ghost woman was gone.

'Tommy?" Mama said.

I ran to the window, but I saw nothing but my reflection. The towel had fallen from my head and my hair hung in wet clumps around my face. My eyes looked like an animal's. I opened the front door. A bat lay on the porch, skull crushed. "Perfect! See what you're doing? The rodents are flying into the windows." I slammed the door.

Mama and Jay/Dad hung like meat carcasses against the wall. "Somebody say something!" I walked past them, for the moment vowing never to look at either one of them again. "Mother! Father!

All this for Tommy." I was out of anger. "All this for Tommy."

They still didn't speak. Mama appeared to have calmed a bit, while Jay/Dad fidgeted with his beard. "Tommy is a murderer, Mama. A murderer. You still love him. How is that? How is it that you can still love him, but you turn your back on us?"

"I never turned my back on you." Both Jay/Dad and I were surprised to hear her speak. "Your father walked out on me. Before I could even tell him. He took the truth and ran away. I stayed, Hannah. Me. I stayed with you. No matter what you might think of me, remember that. I stayed."

My breath hurt. The woman across from me did not resemble my mother. Not the woman who told me to be still and keep my mouth shut. Not the woman who wandered through the house at midnight talking to the dust. Not the woman who told me not to sing like the coloreds.

I stepped over the broken bat on the porch. "I'm gone."

Dear Jay,

I tried, sort of, but I can't really call you Dad, now, can I? I thought not.

I guess we're not going to New York. I mean, that would be a little weird. I can't decide if I want you to stay or go. Mama is talking now, which is different, but I don't understand what she's saying. It's as if she doesn't know what time it is anymore and she's just float-ing away somewhere. Did you love her? Why didn't you stay? Why couldn't you and Mama have worked it out?

How could you have left me all alone in this place? You knew how haunted it was.

Hannah

12
Redemption Day

Roberta du Bois

"I never thought I'd see the day," I said.

Gabriel stood beside me, lips wrapped around a corncob pipe.

"Don't you have anything to say about this?"

We were watching Hannah, Lillian and Jay in a triangle in the living room. Little bits of truth leaked out from all of them, but mostly all three of them stood stiff in their righteousness. Only I saw the unsaid crimes hanging upside down like possums.

"This is the last step," Gabriel said. "I've got work to do."

"What kind of work?"

Hannah stormed off to her room.

"I should go be with her," I said.

"No," said Gabriel. "Stay and watch."

Gabriel looked intently at Jay.

"I don't gather he can see you," I said.

"Nah. That's OK though. I don't need him to see me. I need him to feel me."

Lillian lifted her right hand to cover her mouth, but stopped midway. "Say it!" I said to myself. "Say it!" But as always, she chose silence. "Sometimes, Gabriel, I think if we weren't here in these walls, the whole house would collapse."

Gabriel took his pipe out of his mouth. "You think this house is standing?"

Jay had gone outside. Lillian stood alone in the womb of her house. Her arm still hadn't fallen completely to her side. Frozen again. Jay must have left the door open when he left. A gust of warm wet wind blew through the house. Lillian lowered her arm. "It's getting cold in here," she said.

Gabriel tugged at my sleeve. "We've got to go. The rest is up to her."

I haven't had much of a yearning to go far from this place. Not since Hannah took me to school for show and tell. For all its sorrows, I loved the familiar. "Where are we going?"

He was unwrapping the clothesline from the trees out back. "We're going to Charlotte. Tonight."

Lillian sat on the edge of her marble coffee table. She'd have never sat there unless she was really in a pickle. Her weight was evenly distributed on both feet, her back as straight as a railroad tie. I thought if I blew on her, she'd crumble into dust. Maybe that's what I should have done. Then at least I'd know someone who loved her took her all the way home.

Gabriel wrapped the coil of clothesline around his shoulder. "Time's wasting. We best move along."

I picked up the dead bat from the porch. Its wound was a clean break. "I have to stay here, Gabriel." Lillian stared at the air in front of her. "This one's mine."

"Suit yourself," and he and the clothesline were gone.

Gabriel Wilson
1976

At 12:01 a.m., I showed Tommy what the dark things were. Mr. Janus, the night custodian, had made his rounds. The head nurse read an old issue of *Life* magazine at the front desk. Tommy slept in his single bed in the center of his room. On the nightstand was a reading lamp, a red-covered Bible, an orange cup half-filled with water, and a black ballpoint pen. The fluorescent light on the wall above his bed pulsed green.

I entered his room the same way I did every night, through his dreams. Long scaly fingers reaching into his brain matter, misfiring synapses, reconstructing images. This night, I was careful to be slow. I poured ink made from blackberries into his ears. He didn't move. I pulled a page out of his Bible and made paper cuts beneath each of his fingernails. He batted me away as if I was a ball of yarn and he was a blind kitten. With each exhale, his lower lip flopped loosely. His Adam's apple bounced. I blew on his face. His eyelids stuttered and opened.

I slid along his arms until his fingers gripped the top sheet and held it tight against his neck.

Eenie meenie miney mo

His mouth opened, his tongue a thick black organism, limp against his teeth. "You," he breathed.

Me.

Catch a nigger by the toe.

I slipped behind his skull, lapping at the sides of his neck with my tongue. He clung tighter to the sheet, moved it closer to his face. I swam through the bars of his arms and tapped his belly.

He twisted.

Panted.

Stretched the sheet across his face.

When he inhaled, the sheet pressed against his mouth in an "o." I moved down under the covers between his legs around his feet against his belly. Slide. Scream. Slither.

"No!" he said, slapping at his body.

I laughed, dove into his bellybutton, wrapped around his heart and squeezed.

If he hollers, let him go.

I stretched up through his esophagus, tickling the back of his throat with truth.

"Get out!" he screamed. "Go away!"

He pressed the sheet against his neck. I released his heart, climbed over his ribs and pushed through his chest. Gently, slowly, I kissed his cheek, wet with sweat, sticky with ink. He struggled to move, but his own hands pinned him against the pillow. His own hands, twisting, squirming, slinking, wrapped the bedding around his neck. His own actions pulled the sopping sheet tight around his throat. His beating heart remembered, surrendered, stopped. I never needed the clothesline. His hands released and his head tipped slightly left. Murky ink bubbled out his ears.

I closed his eyes with my breath.

13
What Are Little Girls Made Of

Lillian Green
1976

The inhabitants of the Charlotte State Hospital were sleeping when I arrived after the four-hour drive from the coast. I had ridden in silence the entire trip, fighting with a desire to turn the radio on to drown out the cricking sounds in my head, but ultimately deciding I should punish myself for everything in the whole world by being alone and quiet with myself. I didn't think about Jay on the drive. I thought, believe it or not, mostly about Mother and the last time she and I came to visit Tommy together. I was nineteen then—an official old maid as far as Mother was concerned. We'd spent most of the drive as we spent most of our time together, in a strained silence contained only by the steel in the car doors. When we reached Lumberton we had to wait for a train to cross. No one was behind us. The white and black railroad safety arms formed a wall in front of us. The warning bell must have stirred the ghosts awake.

"I know you saw what Tommy did," Mother said.

The clanging bell grew louder. I was aware of a tingling in the tip of each of my fingers.

"I know you snuck out of the house that night while me and your daddy were fighting." Mother's white-gloved fingers gripped the steering wheel as if it would run away. A string of train cars—coal cars, Santa Fe boxcars, B&N cars—passed in front of us. I could catch the ladder of one of the cars with my mind and head on to Richmond, or maybe even as far away as Pittsburgh.

"I don't need to know details. But I do need to know."

"Yes, Mother. I snuck out."

"That's not what I need to know." She rolled up her window and motioned for me to do the same.

"It's ninety degrees," I said.

"No matter. Just for a moment. Your daddy told me Tommy was set up to take the fall because Daddy had political ambitions. He told me Bob Baker's people did it because your daddy was getting too high in the polls. Bob Baker, well, he was Klan, you know."

Did she not know Daddy was Klan too? Even when I tumbled down the stairs in the sheet with the empty cut-out eyes? Didn't she feel it watching her from inside the closet?

"Bob Baker was Klan." Her grip tightened even more. "He was."

I nodded. I saw no end to the train.

"Well?"

I turned my head as far away from her as I could. Sunflowers danced along the roadside. A few violets remained. "Tommy did it, Mother." I'd always thought I would cry when I finally said those words. But they fell out of me already dead.

A man in a blue and white striped hat stood on the running board of the caboose, waving. The clanging stopped. It would be a few moments before the gate lifted and we could move forward. Mother rolled her window down. Her lips had disappeared into her face. I hadn't told her anything she didn't already know, but somehow it's worse when someone else sets loose the words. Then it takes a mighty strong constitution to stuff them back inside.

Mother succeeded. "Bob Baker was Klan. Not your father." We accelerated. "Not your father."

Not my brother, either.

Lillian Green
1976

The head nurse, unwilling to leave her magazine, beckoned me back with just a hand gesture. I thought of my high school as I walked down the darkened hallway toward Tommy's room. Same institutional construction. Same sense of foreboding. The sense that the walls know something we'll never know. I passed by Mr. Janus, the janitor. "Evenin',"

He touched his cap. "Evenin', ma'am." His gaze lingered on me, possibly just the nocturnal yearning for company. He'd been a good companion for Tommy. Sometimes when Tommy would tell me about the dark things that came to him in the night, he'd say Mr. Janus came by too, afterward, and gave him spearmint gum to quiet the rising bile in his throat. "Mr. Janus sees them too," Tommy said to me once. "He knows I'm not making it up."

"I come to see Tommy," I said.

He nodded. "Gets loneliest at night, I believe."

"I believe so too."

He resumed mopping the floor in overlapping circles, moving the orange cone a foot or two farther away every few mop strokes. Tommy's room was five more doors down on the left. I was surprised to find him in bed when I walked in. He seemed to always be awake at night and asleep in the daytime whenever he could manage it. "The dark things don't let me sleep," he'd said. "They have tentacles and suction cups and dead dead eyes." I'd never had the heart to tell his doctor about them. Tommy was on enough meds. He needed to see whatever it was he needed to see. "I think the dark things are sins, Lillian," he'd said. "I got more of them than anyone else here."

I walked over to the bed, thinking I'd just sit beside him until morning came, and then I'd tell him all about Jay and Hannah and everything that had happened since he did his sin and I did mine and we all fell apart. But when I got closer to the bed, I knew there'd be no more talking.

The smell of Pine-Sol crept under the door. Mr. Janus was moving closer, singing.

Way down yonder in the graveyard walk
I thank God I'm free at last

A clothesline was a coiled snake at the foot of his bed. Tommy's face was wet and still, his neck tattooed with a black circle. The Dixie cup of medication was still full on his nightstand. Half of a piece of spearmint gum was beside it.

Me and my Jesus going to meet and talk
I thank God I'm free at last

Tommy. More dead words were about to fall from my mouth. I thought it odd that Tommy's eyes were already closed. "Rest in peace," I said in spite of myself, in spite of knowing better than most folks, that there's no such thing.

I never went back inside my house. When I got back from Charlotte, I sat behind the steering wheel thinking about what all I thought I knew.

The woman in the walls told me about the slaves that bled right in the spot where my dishwasher is today. She told me about the voices, the breaths trapped in the trees. She told me about the quilt made by the slaves in my family and baby Faith, who only lived to be twenty-three before she was found dead along a riverbank. She told me about Jonathan and the siren girls and how loud, how very loud, this land was. She told me how the snakebite felt and how she knew before she knew that she would not die. She showed me where Claudia was raped and where the big house stood before it was burned. The woman in the walls never could tell me anything about my own mother and my own brother and all the darkness we heaped on everything we touched. She never told me a thing about that. That was mine, she'd said. She could only talk about what was hers. Each body got its own.

Inside my house, Jay and Hannah sat apart.

"He's waiting down by the creek," said the woman living in the walls. "He's been waiting a long time."

I didn't have to ask who. I began to walk.

I hoped my only daughter and my only lover would keep each other safe.

I had seen the triad of water moccasins almost a year before I stuck my foot in Snaky Swamp and called to them with the twirling of my toes. I hoped they would slide quickly around my ankle and pull me under. They didn't, of course, and I had to ease my body into the sucking water inch by inch. The brown eyes that had followed me since 1949 watched me from the tallest pine tree.

Eenie meenie miney mo

My brother killed a black man named Gabriel Wilson in 1949 and his eyes and that rhyme and the silence have never left me. The eyes floated out above the water. I reached out my hand, noticed my mother's aquamarine engagement ring, slipped it off and released it to the swamp.

"Tell." The eyes blinked.

I'm so sorry.

"Tell."

The water was cold and heavy around my bare foot. I eased

my other foot into the swamp. The ground was damp beneath my legs. The houses, my houses, my childhood house and my grown-up house only yards away from each other behind me, seemed to stretch around me in all directions. Their porch columns expanded and wrapped around my body, pinning my arms to my sides.

I loved you so. Tommy. Jay. Hannah.

"Tell."

Mother's quilt, made from generations of slave clothes, created a patchwork family that covered me with its whispers. Hannah can care for it now. Maybe one day she'll want to remember me.

Gabriel. I have never been able to forget you.

"Tell."

There was no wind to echo back my response.

Eenie meenie miney mo

I am an old woman now, Gabriel. I never thought I'd be in this place. Here, in front of you with my hands open. Gabriel, look at me. Here I am at the end of my life and there is only this swamp between us. There's just you and me and all the things that have been.

Look, Gabriel, my hands are open.

The eyes moved next to me and I sat, shoulder to shoulder, with him. Hands spread across my neck. My breathing quickened. The fingers held there, tightening and releasing. I saw a slither in the swamp. Ten fingers became twenty became forty. I opened my mouth.

No noise.

No.

Noise.

The hands pushed me flat onto the ground. An earthworm lay next to my face. From the corner of my eye, I saw a cigarette butt, rimmed with pink lipstick. Deep. Deeper into the earth. Eyes hovered above me now. Above them, a girl with gold hair danced in circles. Round and round, her white dress blurring into clouds. I smelled salt.

"See that boat out there, Butter Bean?"

The golden haired girl stopped, nodded, spun again.

"One day I'm going to buy you your very own boat."

I love you, Tommy.

"I love you, Butter Bean."

The girl vanished. I was in the swamp up to my waist. Three snakes waited, eyes cracking the surface of the water. My heart was strangely still. The eyes moved through the wake of the twirling girl and dove into the water. Forty fingers released their grip on my neck. I choked, inhaled. There was the sailboat and the blue blue water. I saw the truth with my eyes closed.

Eenie meenie miney mo

Let me go.

Hands again on the back of my neck. Falling forward into the water. Snakes' tongues rough as wood. Bending, a sideways "V", into myself. Hands pushed deeper, harder. I tumbled, marsh grass sweeping around my legs. Knotting.

Mouth open.

Scream.

Thick bubbles.

No noise.

No.

no

If he hollers let him go

No more noise.

Bubbles rose around my face. I opened my eyes and saw the black scales on the tail of one of the snakes just beneath my nose. I would have never thought the water was so clear underneath the surface. I breathed in the swamp. Breathed in Mother, Daddy, Tommy, the woman living in my walls, baby Faith, Claudia, Annie, Hannah, sweet Jay, and of course, Gabriel. The marsh grasses tugged. I didn't feel the first bite, fangs as precise as syringes, or the second. It was the third bite I noticed, at the same time the bubbles stopped rising and the weight of the water above me and the pressure of the water below me convinced me that, for the first time, I was flying.

14
Sinking Sand

Roberta du Bois

I watched Lillian's body from beneath the tree. I wanted to pull her out from the water, but I knew it wasn't my place. I knew when the swamp had eaten enough it would let her go. And when that happened, Hannah would find her. It was how it should be, but it didn't stop me from thinking about how long my body stayed in the swamp. I'd gotten stuck in swamp grass for thirteen days before Claudia found me and pulled me out with her bare hands.

"Miss Roberta," she said as she pressed the palm of the hand I'd scalded in the teakettle to my cheekbone. "Lord, Miss Roberta, what you gone and done?"

She didn't cry for me, though. I was waiting for it. Literally wrapped around her neck hoping to taste the salt. She sat with me, picking grass and bugs out of my hair, until Lorita found her.

"It's the mistress," said Claudia. "She gone to meet her Maker."

"Maker don't take nobody who comes on her own terms," said Lorita. "We best get her ready if she's gonna have any chance."

They carried me, these two women whom I had owned. Never once did they try to cover their nose, though I can scarcely imagine how bad the smell was. We went to the grove of trees, which has since been swallowed by the swamp, where we had buried the box of rocks.

"I ain't been back here since," said Claudia.

"No matter," said Lorita. "We put her here."

Claudia's back tensed. "We got to tell Master first."

Lorita stood tall, a tree herself. "We ain't. He ain't looking, he ain't needing to know."

They worked into the night, running back and forth between the big house and the grove. Annie came when she could with a linen tablecloth to wrap me in. Jonathan rocked in the porch swing drinking whiskey from the bottle. My father sat across from him on the bench. Neither man had been looking for me. If I had been a runaway slave, they'd have been out searching all day.

"Times are getting tense," my father said.

Jonathan nodded, lilting a little to the left.

"You can't let up on anything. Not now."

Jonathan nodded again. "Nothing."

"Trouble's coming," my father said. "Trouble the likes of which we haven't seen before. You have to be prepared to do whatever is necessary. There's talk of secession."

"Sesshhesshun," Jonathan slurred.

"There could be a war anytime. Brother against brother." Annie stepped on a twig on her way back to the house. My father paused. "You seen Roberta lately?"

"No," said Jonathan.

"Hmmm. Reckon she'll be back eventually."

"She's got a temper, you know. Likes to wander off when she gets mad."

Perhaps my father was surprised he spoke a complete sentence. Perhaps it was something else entirely. "Yes, she surely does."

Both men sat in silence while Lorita and Claudia wrapped me in the white linen cloth they'd spackled and pressed a hundred times before.

"Go get Morrey to dig the hole," said Lorita. "I'll stay with her."

Claudia seemed happy to move away from me. Once she was through the thicket of trees, Lorita laid her hands on my chest and hummed so deep I felt the vibration even outside my flesh. She swayed and clucked her tongue and pressed her hands harder on my ribs. I almost wished I was still inside my body, just so I could feel her touch. "You go rest in peace, Miss Roberta. You go rest in peace.

Follow that sound and don't look back."

But I couldn't follow. She was right. The Maker doesn't take anyone who leaves on her own terms.

I wished someone would come and wrap Lillian in linen.

"Someone come soon."

Who's there?

A different voice. "She won't stay there long as you."

"She's alright."

There they were in front of me – white, black, white, black – holding hands in a line.

"I haven't seen you in awhile," I said.

"We here," said Number Two.

"We always here," said Number One.

"Where did she go?" I asked.

"On home," said Number Three. "We give her her song."

"She love you," said Number Two.

"She did," said Number Three.

The sirens crossed onto the pier, sat down and hung their legs over the side.

"I loved her," I said. "I'd have been so lonely."

"Come home now," said Number One.

"Lay your burden down now," said Number Two. "Time has come."

"We could sing for you," said Number Three.

Could I go where Lillian went?

"Water baptize you," said Number Two.

"Wash everything away," said Number One.

I laughed. "Not the last time. The water just made everything sticky."

"Last time you run to us. This time we come to you. That make all the difference," said Number Two.

I tilted my head. Hannah was coming. Three of the sirens vanished. Number Four stayed put on the pier, never taking her eyes off me.

Hannah Green
1976

I found my mother. I was walking by the creek when I saw a swarm of flies over the water. Sometimes dead birds floated on the surface, so I was expecting a heron or maybe an owl's body. I saw her hand first, bloated, ripped skin hanging on her bones. Even then, I didn't think it was Mama. She'd been missing for two days, but we assumed she'd gone to Charlotte to visit Tommy. To tell the truth, I didn't care where she went. I didn't care where Jay/Dad went or where anyone went. I wanted only to be alone to try and erase everything that happened. I had decided I was going to go on to New York anyway and find my own record deal.

When I got closer to the water, I saw her face. Her once blue eyes were open, but the sockets were picked apart by fish and snakes. Her lips had separated, making her cheeks look stretched, rotten. She wasn't too far from the marsh-edge of the water. I broke off a branch from a pine tree and reached out for her. At first, I pushed her farther out, but I walked onto the pier and was able to hook the stick through the pocket on her dress and pull her towards me.

I knelt on the splintered wood and when she was close enough, I reached under her arms and pulled her onto the platform. I was surprised by how heavy she was. I breathed steadily for a few minutes and then sat beside her, covering my nose with my left hand. With my right hand, I pulled leaves out of her thin yellow hair and traced the outline of her eyebrows. The flies were glassy green and had wings etched with veins. They liked her eye sockets and her ears. Wet grass clung to her ankles and calves, twisting between her bare toes like fingers.

"Mama," I said, my voice foreign and too loud. I picked up her hand, tried to fold the skin flaps back over the bone. Her fingernails were deeply ridged. More flies came as the sun set, and the slurp of water against the posts of the pier sounded like strangling. "I'd have sung for you, Mama, if you'd heard."

Crickets celebrated nightfall. My clothes dried clammy on my skin. Mama dripped water back into the creek. Across the road, I heard children laughing. But I could have imagined it. I could have imagined this whole thing, but the body next to me was so silent it raged. I thought I saw a pair of brown eyes watching out over the water. Looked like the same pair of brown eyes I thought I saw after singing in the choir. A girl could creep herself out here, sitting on the pier in the dark with the dripping body of her mother. Frogs began their deep honking cries. I was cold.

"Mama."

Jay/Dad found us both, hours later, in the moonlight, and the sound he made reminded me of a coon dog, circling round and round a tree, catching nothing.

I had nothing I could sing for her now that she was gone. I felt like I should have already had something prepared, you know, like a good daughter would. When I pulled her from the creek I did feel something besides rage, which had been the biggest piece of feeling I'd had lately. But I don't know as you could call anything swishing through my veins love. I wanted to call it love. Maybe love is really nothing more than sticking with someone long enough to know when it's time to bury them and move on.

I went right to my room after Jay/Dad found us. He could take care of calling the undertaker. He was the grown-up. When I got to my room, the ceiling had slanted into someone else's room. Some woman who sang other people's music while she waited for a break. Some woman who wrote average poetry and called it good. Some woman who still had a chance to love her mother. Even my bed was someone else's. I was too big for it now, and the quilt underneath me too light to hold me.

"You know that quilt comes from my days."

"Jay?"

"Me, darling. Over here."

She was more transparent than I'd ever seen her, perched in the straight-backed desk chair. Through her sternum, I could see the picture of the Okracoke Island Lighthouse that hung on my wall by the window.

"Your mama was my friend, you know."

I didn't want to talk. Not now. Not to her.

"She was the first one to see me. It was quite a relief to me, let me tell you. I thought I was going to wander through these walls forever with no one ever looking up from their devil's food cake to take note."

"This house is cursed," I said and started to cry not for Mama, but for the house. It was just boards and nails and shingles and paint. It didn't deserve us.

"Your mama thought that too, you know. Something you two have in common."

"Doesn't matter much now, does it?"

"Hard to believe that quilt managed to hold up so well all these years."

I ran my hands across it, each square a new bump. "It's been on my bed as long as I can remember."

"Your mama's bed before that."

"Then where?"

"Your mama's mama."

"Grandmother never struck me as someone who'd care too much about saving things."

Roberta laughed. "You're right about that. But this mattered. This was where she came from. It's where you come from too."

"And where's that?"

Roberta paused then. I thought she was going to vanish and leave me there all alone. But she didn't. "The blood of lots of people," she said finally. "Theirs and mine. Lots of blood, any way you look at it. Makes for a messy family."

Understatement of the year. I didn't hear any more noise from the front of the house. Maybe Jay/Dad went back to New York. Maybe he figured he had the best opportunity he'd be likely to get in the near future to sneak out of here with no words to any of us.

"We all gave something to that quilt, whether we wanted to or not." She touched a faded blue square. "See that here? That's from my husband Jonathan. He wore that shirt practically every day until I couldn't mend it anymore. He wore that fabric out. And this one here – " she touched a square of purple velvet – "is from the cover we wrapped the Bible in. We didn't waste anything. Not a thing." She tucked her hands under her chin. "Wonder where that Bible went."

"I wrote letters to her, you know."

"I know."

"I thought one day she'd see them. I left them right out in the open for her."

"Sometimes it's hardest to see what's right in front of our eyes, child," she said. A snake, wrapped around the brim of her hat, stuck a forked tongue between its lips. "Your mama went to hear you sing at the waterfront. Did you know that?"

"Don't tell me that now."

"She did though. And when she came back, she danced in the living room. I watched her. She twirled and twirled and collapsed on the sofa like she'd found religion. You gave her music, Hannah-girl. You did."

Jay/Dad and I stood beside each other at Mama's gravesite. Only the two of us had come to see her put in the ground. Pastor Thomas had already gone back to the church. He had leaned on a walker while reciting the prayers.

"I hope your mother finds peace with God," he said, clutching my wrist with his liver-spotted fingers. "I do know she never found it here."

I looked at the old man, new venom rising in my throat, but I smiled. "Thank you."

The graveyard was on a slight incline in back of Cornerstone Southern Baptist Church. Buttercups and the palest purple violets grew around the base of the graves. Ancient willow trees bent mossy arms over the tombs. The day was overcast and the wind off the ocean was cold. I wore an ankle-length black silk dress and a white scarf. The scarf was not heavy enough to keep me warm. Jay/Dad was kind of handsome in a black suit with a crimson tie. I could tell by the way he walked that his dress shoes pinched his feet. I had chosen cherry wood for Mother's coffin. Part of me wanted the cheaper pine box, but in the end I couldn't hate her enough to deprive her bones of satin bedding. The casket was closed, resting on a wooden bier. The gravedigger sat a few rows over, whittling, whistling under his breath.

"Ready to go on home now?" Jay/Dad asked.

"Did you love her?"

The gravedigger thought we were moving and stood up. Jay/Dad held out his hand to stop him. "Always." He spit on the earth, then cupped my face in his hands. "Did you?"

"Always."

He began to whistle and then he sang, "Should auld acquaintance be forgot and never brought to mind?"

I almost giggled. "What's that about?"

"I sang that for your mother on our first date," he said, then grabbed my shoulders from behind me. "Sing with me."

"I can't."

He whistled slow. "Should auld acquaintance be forgot and days of Auld Lang Syne."

"For Auld Lang Syne, my dear, for Auld Lang Syne," I spoke-sang, remembering the incident in church.

He took my hand. "That's my girl."

Together. "We'll take a cup of kindness yet, for Auld Lang Syne."

The gravedigger watched us from behind a headstone.

Jay/Dad tapped on the coffin lid with his knuckles. I took two steps back. I heard his inhaling breath before he pressed his forehead against the lid, shook, and rose again. We walked in silence back to our house.

Roberta du Bois

In 1865, after the War, no one cared how loud Jonathan du Bois screamed. The siren girls and I watched from the swamp. No one heard what Claudia whispered in his ear before she took the poker from the fireplace and pressed it into his thigh. No one heard his high-pitched begging as she turned him over and branded her initials on his spine. No one heard her voice soothe him "this won't hurt at all" each time the white-hot metal seared his flesh. The siren girls and I swung from the vines and cheered, silent as the ghosts we always knew we were.

Hannah Green
1976

The fine gray sand felt cool to my feet, even though the fall afternoon was unusually warm. No sign of Mama's spirit disappearing over the dunes. Still, I walked toward the east, toward the sea, toward the place I used to come when I was a girl to wait for my mythical father to appear, a phoenix, glorious and immortal.

The wind blew stronger the closer I got to the ocean. I wished I'd changed into jeans. I still carried the brine from the swamp on my skin. The shrieks of the gulls beckoned me. Faster! Faster! I began to run. The pins in my hair fell out and my hair streamed around my shoulders and down my back. I ran my hand through it, loosening the tangles as I picked up speed. The dune seemed steeper than usual. I'd walked them, looking for my father, countless times. My side ached and I began to run in angles, my feet cutting tracks in the smooth sand.

When I reached the top of the tallest dune, I stopped. I saw my house, small as a child's toy, to my right. To my left was the very edge of Snaky Swamp. The snakes had taken it back. They wriggled and writhed on top of each other, waves of scales and spines. Behind me was the outline of the township of Alderman. A thin haze covered the landscape. I saw the grocery store, the church steeple, the mayor's house—"should have been your grandaddy's house," Mama would say—but only because I knew they were there. In front of me, the glorious ocean sparkled. The yellow light splashed off the white caps of the low waves as they traveled to shore, creating a golden mosaic. The whoosh of the water as it washed over the sand and returned to itself tugged my tears out.

I scurried down the dune. Midway between the top and the bottom was a crevice, just big enough for two people to sit in. Brown rock worn smooth from wind and water lined the edges.   I stopped, crouched down, and sat, pressing my back against the hard, warm rock. No one was here. Just air.

With every tickle from the ocean breeze across my flesh, I wondered what I should remember of Mama. Now seemed to be the time to make up the stories I could carry with me from this place. Now seemed to be the time to make the mother I always wanted from salt and sand.

The hairs on my arms lifted. I shaded my eyes with my hand and looked around. No one. I dropped my arm to my lap and leaned back against the rock. Perhaps I'd see her down by the shore searching for sand dollars or washed up wreckage.

I knew I could sit on this rock until the moon rose as high as the sun and still I would not see anything. Not the light. Not the ships. Not the stories. Not, especially not, my mother walking towards me.

Instead, I saw what I've always seen. Roberta and Gabriel dancing to the beat of the waves. Did they usher her out? Was anyone there for her at all? Dear Mama. Dear Mama. I'm so sorry you'll never be anything else but dead. Our time has passed.

Dad—Jay—said he'd hang around a spell. I can't believe that, though. Maybe someday.

I don't think Roberta and Gabriel see me anymore. They're beautiful, dancing like that so close to the ocean. The pink from her hat kissing the brown of his cheek. The tentacles of the foam wrapping their feet together. Maybe that's as close as any of us ever get to the ghost dance of love.

Tide was coming in. I wondered what it wouldn't swallow next.

Dear Mama,

    I was born into a house of ghosts. I grew up with one foot with the living and one foot with the dead. At the time, I hated it. I resented the dead things, the dead wishes, the dead hopes and of course, the dead people that flowed through our house like wind. You made sure the ghosts stayed. All those dead things, you'd think you'd have become a ghost too. But I have listened for you in the trees, and I have looked for you in the walls, and I don't hear or see anything. Just like when you were here, I guess. I couldn't find you then and I can't find you now.

    The difference is I think sometimes I'd like to find you now. Maybe I could find a song we both could sing.

    I miss you, Mama, and I did love you.

    I think maybe you loved me too, a little bit. As much as there was room for in your heart that you'd stuffed with Tommy and silence. I hope wherever you are now, that you are talking.

    Hannah

15
Exhalations

The Swamp Sirens

"Is she coming?" asked Number Three.

"I don't know," said Number Two. "Could she be ready?"

"Now's the time! Now's the time!" said Number One. "Grab my hands!"

Number Two and Number Three took Number One's hands. "Make a ring!" said Number One. "She's coming home!"

Ring around the rosies
Pocket full of posies
Ashes, ashes
We all fall down!

Number Four sat on the highest branch of the tree, swinging her dark legs. "She's not coming yet."

"She is! She is!" said Number One. "You've got to come make a circle."

"Too dark still for her," Number Four said. "Still too dark."

"Maybe we could sing her home," said Number Three.

They watched Roberta watch the swamp. They caught each breath she exhaled in their mouths and held it.

"She's so lonely," said Number Two.

"So lonely."

"Lonely, lonely."

The three sirens separated their circle and waited for Number Four.

"It has to be all of us," said Number Three.

"Yes, all of us," said Number One. "She's ready."

Number Four hadn't exhaled Roberta's breath back to her.

"You've got to let her go too," said Number Three. "What are you holding on to?"

Number Four shook her head, slipped through the noose hanging just below her.

Number Three sat on the ground beneath the tree, pale arms crossed over her chest. "It has to be all of us."

Number Four looked over the top of Roberta's feathered hat, out to the ruins of what had been Idyllic Grove Rice Plantation. She looked behind Roberta and saw Gabriel waiting, his work now done. Number Four saw the frailness of Roberta's ancient heart beating, softer with each moment, in the cage of her ribs.

"She feels it now," said Number Two.

"She's coming back in," said Number One. "Gabriel's coming too! We've got to get ready to catch them when they cross!"

"New day! New day!" Number Two held her dark arms above her head, yellow pinafore swaying on her hips.

Number Four exhaled loud and fierce enough to move the branches. Roberta choked. Gabriel stayed steady.

Number Three started singing. "Who are these children all dressed in red?"

"God's a-gonna trouble the water," sang Number Two.

"Must be the children that Moses led."

"God's a-gonna trouble the water."

Number One jumped in. "Wade in the water! Wade in the water, children! Wade in the water!"

One, Two and Three joined hands. "God's a-gonna trouble the water."

Number Four moved closer, parted her lips. "If you get there before I do."

The sirens held their arms up, fingers intertwined, to the top of the tree. A bat flew through the circle of limbs, looking to Roberta for all the world like an angel of God. She touched the scar on her neck where the snake had bitten her over a century ago. Gabriel felt the burning of the snake around his neck where the rope had sunk. The black water undulated against the posts of the pier. There was no moon. The clearest things they saw were the shadows in the water.

Roberta looked back at the house. Sweet Hannah inside, mourning. Lillian, now in the ground. The house, standing as tall as ever, vines stretched between the posts, a thorny awning over the stairs. No more smoke from the chimney. No more hogs in the yard. Baby Faith, gone on home.

Gabriel looked back at the house. Fourteen-year-old Lillian saw him bleed. He spat into the swamp. His mouth was hot, unfresh. His bare feet chilled from the water.

Eenie meenie miney mo.

Roberta grabbed his hand. Her blue eyes affected him. Four-teen-year-old Lillian's eyes. So very blue.

"If it could be undone...." Her grip hurt him.

"It cannot."

She released his hand. Blood drained from two pinholes in her neck. "It hurts."

"Yes."

"I didn't remember."

"I did."

Gabriel's neck tightened. He had trouble breathing. His flesh swelled. His hands grew dry.

"I didn't remember the water being so black." Roberta knelt on the pier, her hand dangling in the cold water. The blood on her neck attracted flies. Gabriel knelt beside her. The house was in back of them. In front of them, the creek that flowed to the Inland Water-way that flowed to the Atlantic that flowed home.

"Crossroads right here," said Gabriel.

Roberta's lips moved. "God's a-gonna trouble the water."

All four sirens joined hands, dark on light, light on dark. "Tell all my friends I'm coming too!"

"God's a-gonna trouble the water," sang Gabriel.
Wade in the water.
Wade in the water, children.
Wade in the water.
God's gonna trouble the water.

A creature came up for air, cracking the still surface of the water. Roberta gasped. Gabriel could no longer remain upright. He curled into himself on the edge of the pier, his head pressed against his knees. Roberta turned to see the house once more, but it had vanished. All she saw were acre upon acre of pines. An owl shrieked.

Ring around the rosies.
Eenie meenie miney mo.

Gabriel raised his head enough to see the flesh on Roberta's face dissolve. The blue of her eyes still struck his heart. It thumped once. Twice. He reached for her and she responded, grasping his hand with all her remaining strength as they leapt from the pier, tumbling in perfect somersaults into the waiting water.

The author gratefully acknowledges:

The Barbara Deming Award for Women for early support of this work; Soapstone: A Writing Retreat for Women for space and time to imagine; Antioch University Los Angeles; Alma Luz Villanueva for breathing life into the early drafts; Jim Krusoe for the bird scene; Carol Anne Perini for our first writer's group and for believing I was a writer; Gayle Brandeis for our writing retreat in Venice Beach and for reading endless drafts of this book; Linda Roghaar for first seeing this project as possible; Jennifer Urban-Brown for editorial assistance; Mary Sojourner for friendship and early draft advice; Arvin Loudermilk and Mike Iverson for visual clarity; Jeffrey Hartgraves for staging the first reading of this work in San Francisco; Connell Scruggs Herring for financial support; Gus Brett for unflinching belief in my writing; My mother, Elinor, for staying; and Keith Haynes for his constant love and friendship.

An Interview With Laraine Herring

Where did the inspiration for Ghost Swamp Blues come from?

I began *Ghost Swamp Blues* through the voice of Lillian, loosely modeled on my grandmother, in an attempt to understand her and find some way to connect with her. I invented the situation which became Lillian's inciting incident—witnessing her brother Tommy lynch Gabriel. I followed that thread—what would happen if a young girl saw that? How would she be affected? What secrets would she keep? What detachments would be necessary? From that initial question, that first attempt to reconcile myself with my now deceased family, the novel took form.

Growing up in the south, I witnessed many deeply divisive belief systems. I saw Klan rallies, nice church-going women throwing rocks at the buses that brought the black children into our schools in the 1970s, and watched as our "friendly" neighborhood stopped speaking to us and literally built fences between our home and theirs when we sold our house to an African-American family.

As I became engulfed by the melody of *Ghost Swamp Blues*, I asked deeper questions. What price is paid by the dominant culture in an environment of dominance? In other words, what is the soul price for an individual who owns another? What songs and shadows still cling to the land? This novel is my journey to understand the shadow of my family, my homeland, and the shadow within myself.

Can you tell us something about your writing process?

I usually begin with a place and a voice. So far, I've never begun with a story or plot. It's always been a place and a sound. Someone will speak to me or make some sort of noise, whether it's dragging a shoe across a wooden pier, or an actual line of dialogue. For *Ghost Swamp Blues*, the first thing I got was a woman in a pink feathered hat walking into a swamp. The rest of the book unfolded from that image and that place. From there, I got Lillian's voice. "I stopped speaking when...." I was curious. I wanted to know why she stopped speaking. What happened? And the desire to answer those questions brought me the story. I am one of those writers who has no idea where she's going until she gets there. I'm not an outliner or plot constructor. I listen and follow, and then later have to shape the elements I discover into a workable narrative.

This novel went through many different incarnations before finding its current form. Please talk to us about the revision process.

I actually began this novel in 1998 when I started my MFA program. My grandmother had recently died and family history was on my mind. I workshopped the novel to death in grad school; a section of the book won the Barbara Deming Award for Women, and I successfully landed an agent with this book. However, it has taken a decade to find the perfect home for it. Along the way, I rewrote it as a young adult novel, then I rewrote it with an omniscient narrator, and then ended up cutting what I had thought was an integral plot point, after discovering that it didn't matter and in fact, the absence of it made the book stronger.

I love the revision process. It's every bit as exciting to me as the early drafts. I am a scratch rewriter, meaning I start over without the earlier version in front of me. That way, I don't have the earlier words getting in the way of the words that could come. Each full revision honed me in tighter on the focus of the book. Each version taught me something new about the characters and brought into deeper clarity my driving questions and my character arcs.

You write and teach a lot about using writing as a healing tool. Many people may associate that type of writing only with personal journaling. How do you think fiction writing can serve as a healing tool?

I think all of our stories spring from unresolved questions within ourselves. It takes a lot of discipline and stamina to write a book. If you as the author are not curious or compelled by the questions the book is posing, you'll find something better to do with your time. We don't always know, or need to know, the questions we're pursuing in our work. Sometimes I think it's better if we don't know at all and just step back and listen to the work. If we think we know too much, there's a tendency to also think we know the answers. That can be deadly in the writing process. Trust the work. It will reveal to you far more than you could have directed it to.

The questions each of us carry through our lives come from some level of life's experience. Prior to teaching creative writing, I would not have felt that fiction writing was as healing for the author as journaling or other more therapeutic types of writing. But once I started to read my students' stories and listen to what they were examining through their characters, I could see the deeper questions at play in their own lives. In some ways, because people think they're "making it up," they're able to be more authentic and honest because they don't see the personal connection yet. It's there. It's always there.

People can write themselves free. Writing writes us free. Once we get out of our own way, the stories, the unresolved questions, the trauma we store, wants to move and be liberated. This is only one of the many ways the pen is mightier than the sword. Writing and reading in any genre teach us empathy for ourselves and the world around us. Empathy leads to compassion. Compassion leads to a softening. When we soften, we can let go of what we no longer need. It sounds out there, I know, but I see it semester after semester in my students, and I see it project after project with my own work. Writing opens us.

The supernatural figures prominently in this book. Do you believe in ghosts?

I believe places and people can attract and hold onto energies that aren't of the present moment. I have had quite a few encounters in my life that I cannot explain. Were they ghosts? I have no idea. I just know I experienced things I couldn't understand based on how we think the world works. I believe in hauntings. I think we are often the ones who haunt ourselves, rather than something otherworldly, but the effect is the same. Places hold energy, and the South is a living museum to the whole range of what it means to be a human being. I have always been able to feel and hear places. I don't see things as much as hear them. The Southern landscape shouts to me.

Do you consider yourself a Southern writer?

I do. I haven't lived in the South since 1981, and I'm not sure I could live there anymore, but it will always be home. I have tried to write fiction that takes place in Arizona, where I currently live, and I come up empty. I know there are many people who love this desert landscape, but to me, it is too unsafe, too large. The sky is too big. I need the canopy of trees and the softness of grass. I love Southern Gothic stories. I love big crazy family stories, and I love all the contradictions that play out every day in the South. As Southern author Lee Smith says, "In the South, a sense of place implies who you are and what your family did. It's not just literally the physical surroundings, what stuff looks like. It's a whole sense of the past." That's how I feel about the South. The West doesn't give me that. It's not my past. It's someone else's. I believe time wraps around itself rather than moves in a straight line, so it is comforting to me to be in the South, where I can see many layers of different lives in one spot.

Who are some of your favorite authors?

Of course the great Southern writers—Flannery O'Conner, William Faulkner and Truman Capote. I also adore Carole Maso, Toni Morrison, Isabel Allende and Barbara Kingsolver. I think James Agee's novel, *A Death in the Family*, is quite possibly the most perfect book ever written.

Book Group Discussion Questions

1) When Lillian divulges to Jay her secret, that she witnessed Tommy murder Gabriel Wilson, Jay rejects her and holds her responsible for the death of his cousin. Twenty years later, he reiterates her responsibility, saying, "The man your brother killed was my family. You let it happen. You let him die." In your view, can Lillian be held accountable in any sense? Is there any basis to Jay's charge?

2) Several characters in the novel—Annie, Claudia, Lorita—are, literally speaking, slaves. Several scenes are set on the Idyllic Grove Rice Plantation in the 1850s and 1860s. However, slavery can also be metaphorical; people can be trapped by their circumstances and their choices. Are any characters in *Ghost Swamp Blues* enslaved in a metaphorical sense? Are Lillian's mother, father, Lillian and Tommy enslaved in any way? Although Roberta is the plantation mistress, how is she not free? After she becomes a ghost, is she still metaphorically enslaved? At the novel's climax, do Lillian and Gabriel free themselves, Lillian through suicide and Gabriel through revenge? Do their actions liberate any other characters?

3) In literature, a symbol functions on a literal level, serving the needs of a scene or plot, while also suggesting deeper meanings. Discuss what is suggested by the family quilt that Roberta discusses with Hannah following Lillian's death. What is suggested by Tommy and Lillian removing batting from the quilt in earlier scenes?

4) What are some of the parallels between the two sets of characters from the 19th and 20th centuries? For example, how are Jonathan DuBois and Lillian's father similar? How are Roberta and Lillian similar? What are some of the similarities between the 19th and 20th century, between the "old" and "new" Souths?

5) What is suggested in the name of Faith, Hannah's ancestor, and the person who is the literal, ancestral link between the two sets of characters?

6) Throughout the novel there is a theme of silencing. Roberta is silenced by her mother when she objects to marrying Jonathan. Annie and Claudia are silenced by their enslavement and by Roberta's actions (for example, when Roberta places Claudia's hand in the scalding water). Roberta attempts to silence herself by walking into Snaky Swamp. Lillian silences herself after witnessing Tommy's actions. She then silences her daughter, Hannah, when she hears Hannah sing in church. Hannah tries to communicate with her mother, using the non-verbal medium of letters, but receives no response from Lillian. What or who is still left silenced at the end of the novel? What or who is liberated? Why do you think Lillian was so compelled to silence Hannah? What is the significance of Hannah's voice?

7) *Ghost Swamp Blues* is a magical realism novel. The magical elements in the story are treated as normal occurrences. Throughout the book, the supernatural and the ordinary walk side by side. Within the novel, where do the supernatural and the ordinary intersect? Which characters are the primary links between the two worlds? What elements exist in both worlds?

8) What role do the Swamp Sirens play in the book? Are they part of the supernatural world, the natural world, or both?

9) The novel takes place in a mythical North Carolina coastal town on a piece of property that has undergone many incarnations. The constant on the property is the swamp. What role does Snaky Swamp play in the 19th-century portions of the novel? The 20th-century portions? Why do Gabriel and Roberta return to the swamp at the end of the novel?

10) As Roberta enters Snaky Swamp, she is bitten by water moccasins. What do you think the snakes represent for Roberta? For Lillian? For Gabriel?

About The Author

LARAINE HERRING holds an MFA in creative writing and an MA in counseling psychology. She has developed numerous workshops that use writing as a tool for healing grief and loss. She is the author of *The Writing Warrior: Discovering the Courage to Free Your True Voice* (Shambhala), *Writing Begins with the Breath: Embodying Your Authentic Voice* (Shambhala), *Lost Fathers: How Women Can Heal from Adolescent Father Loss* (Hazelden) and *Monsoons: A Collection of Writing* (Duality Press). Her short stories, poems, and essays have appeared in national and local publications. Her fiction has won the Barbara Deming Award for Women and her nonfiction work has been nominated for a Pushcart Prize. She currently teaches creative writing in Prescott, Arizona, and at the Omega Institute in New York and the Kripalu Center for Yoga and Health in Massachusetts.

Learn more about Laraine at
www.laraineherring.com

CPSIA information can be obtained at www.ICGtesting.com
Printed in the USA
BVOW040641151111

276056BV00001B/62/P